Crushed Hope

His Warriors
Book 4

By

Ronna M. Bacon

Psalm 147:11
The LORD delights in those who fear him,
who put their hope in his unfailing love.

Table of Contents

Chapter 1

It was going to be one of those days, Larkin MacTavish thought. The spring day was cold and rainy. Enough already! I want some warm weather, some sunshine. She turned to look around her as she climbed from her car and then reached into the trunk for her briefcase. She had a new client and she just didn't want to be here. She walked up the crumbling walk to the tiny house, her eyes scanning the area out of habit. The white paint was peeling and the steps felt spongy under her shoes.

A knock at the door went unanswered. She knocked again, then pulled out her phone to check her schedule. She was at the right place and at the right time. Now, where was her client?

She stepped off the porch and looked around, her green eyes not missing much. This is so bizarre, she thought. No one home but an appointment clearly scheduled. She dialed her secretary.

"Hi, Eve. It's Larkin. Did anyone call in from the Petty Road address? No? Because I'm here and no one is home. I know. Yes, I think we should. I'll wait here until the patrol car gets here. Call my last client. Let them know I've been delayed for a bit. Hopefully I can still make it today."

Once more her eyes sought the area around the house. It was out in the country, but there were no trees close by it. A crumbling structure behind it must have been a garage at some point, she thought. Now what? Who knows how long it will take the cruiser to arrive? Do I wait, she thought, or do I leave? Lord, I'm scared, more scared than I have been in years, and I don't know why. I feel like there's something hanging over my head, about to fall. So where are You? Can I trust You? Can I place my hope in You once more?

She turned as she heard tires on the gravel driveway and frowned. Not a patrol car. She drew back to her car, hand on the door handle, ready to jump in if she needed to. She watched as the truck parked behind her and a tall younger man climbed down and then walked towards her. She reached for her phone in her pocket, ready to call for help.

The man stopped, watching the young woman in front of him, taking in the deep red of her hair and the sparkling green of her eyes. He ran a hand through his black hair, his deep blue eyes thoughtful.

"Hi! Is there anyone home?" He pointed at the house.

"I don't know. The police are on their way."

The man sighed. Not a good day. He had been given this new client to help with their speech after a stroke and now there wasn't a client at home. Strange, he thought.

He walked towards the young woman, then stopped a few feet from her, watching her apprehension.

"I'm Matthias Strong. I was supposed to meet a client about speech pathology today. You're here for a reason as well?"

Larkin nodded, her eyes studying the man, then the house. "I'm Larkin

MacTavish, occupational therapist. I was to be here as well today. I couldn't get an answer when I knocked."

Matthias looked around. "The place is really rundown, isn't it? Did you try another door?"

Larkin shook her head. "No, I didn't. If I don't get an answer at the front door, I either leave or call for assistance. This client should be home and someone should be with them."

Matthias nodded, then headed around the house. Larkin took a look at him, sighed, and then followed him. He was a stranger to her, but somehow he made her feel safe. Feel safe? She snorted. Now, what was that? She hadn't felt safe in years.

Matthias tapped at the back door, then shielding his eyes with his hands, peeked through the door.

"Do you see anyone?" Larkin's quiet voice came from behind him.

"No. I don't." He stepped back, looking around, then focused on the woman in front of him. "And there should be. Why book both of us today and not cancel if nobody would be here?" He walked away from the house, his eyes once more roving the area. A frown on his face, he headed for the building at the back.

"Hey, wait! We can't walk all over this property!" Larkin stood, hands on her hips, watching him.

"If I think someone's hurt out there, I will. If you're not coming, then go and lock yourself in your car."

Larkin stared at him, then ran to catch up. "You're not a police officer in disguise, are you?"

Matthias laughed, the sound rumbling through Larkin's heart and chipping at the ice that encased it. Why, she wondered, did he have that effect on her?

"No, I'm not. Just a civilian like you. But there is something strange here. I don't like it. How long since you called for help?"

"Twenty minutes? It doesn't surprise me that it would take time for them to come. This would likely be a low priority."

Matthias shook his head. "No, it's not. Not with the relative of this client."

"What do you mean?" Larkin pulled him to a stop.

He stared down at her for a moment. "You have no idea? Do you live in town?"

She nodded. "It's my hometown, but I've been away for a while. Who's the relative?"

"The hospital board chair is a nephew. He would make sure his aunt got help." He stopped as Larkin snorted again. "You don't seem to think so."

"I know the guy. If there was money in it, he would. Other than that, he wouldn't care."

"That sounds harsh." Matthias started walking once more for the decrepit building.

"Trust me. He has a heart of stone although he puts on a good face for the public. My Mom went to school with him. She says he hasn't changed from then, only gotten worse."

Matthias reached out a hand to stop her, his head turned to catch a sound. A sudden revving of a motor had him spinning, trying to find the source and direction. A scream for Larkin had him facing her again as a truck sped towards them from behind the building. He leapt for her, gathering her into his arms, and desperately shoving her away from the truck's path. He landed hard and rolled, his head hitting the ground. They tumbled across the ground and then lay still. The truck stopped for a few seconds and then took off, digging large ruts into the wet ground.

Minutes later, the click of closing doors sounded through the still quiet day. A knock could be heard at the front door, then footsteps sounding as the two officers headed for the back door. A shout and they were running for Matthias and Larkin.

The first officer dropped to his knees for an assessment as the second officer, weapon drawn, searched around the building, then pointed at the house.

Larkin stirred as the EMS worked on her. She squinted as her eyes open.

"What happened?"

"That's what we'd like to know."

She looked at the officer standing there. "Danny? You're here?"

"I am, Larkin. Can you tell me what happened?"

She sighed. "I wish I knew. I was here to meet a client. Matthias arrived. He couldn't get an answer either. We headed back this way to see if someone was here and a truck came at us. Matthias?"

"He's been transported already."

"How is he?"

Danny shook his head. "You know I can't tell you. He's under medical care now."

"Danny! He saved my life. I would have been run down but for him."

"But would you have even been back here if he hadn't come around the building?"

She stared at him and then nodded. "Likely."

He stood, staring down at her, then shook his head. "Give it a rest, Larkin. I'll pass your number on to him. If he wants to contact you, he will."

Larkin sighed, her eyes closing against the headache she had, feeling the stretcher being wheeled towards the front of the yard.

"Danny?" She waited until he turned to her and then approached. "My client?"

"I'm sorry, Larkin. She's not here. No one is. You're sure this is the address you were given?"

"Absolutely. Check with Eve as well. Why would someone give both Matthias and I a wrong address?"

"That's what I want to know. Jason Long's on his way out. He's been asked to help us investigate."

Chapter 2

Matthias groaned as he sat up on the bed in the Emergency Department of the Elmton Hospital. He hurt more than if he had been hit in a football scrimmage. What had happened?

He looked up through bleary eyes as the curtain was pulled back. Jason Long, police detective, stood there.

"Matthias?"

"Jason, what happened?"

"You were almost run down by a truck. Care to explain?"

"It's all blurry. I don't really remember much from when I left my office at noon. So, what happened?"

Jason studied him, then nodded. "You had gone to a new client, didn't get an answer, and headed towards the back of the property to search. A truck almost ran you down."

Matthias nodded. "Was there anyone home?"

Jason stared at him for a moment. "No, there wasn't. It wasn't even an address for the client. So how did you get it?"

"I was called by the hospital. They gave me the address." Matthias held up his hand. "Wait. There was someone else there. Is she all right?"

"Larkin? She's fine, thanks to you. You shoved her out of the way in time. Just some bruises and bumps. She really does want to thank you. Here's her card."

Matthias reached for it, grimacing at the pain. "Thanks, Jason. Now, about that address? How did the hospital get it then?"

"It was an old address. Someone didn't bother to update their records. I've called the client's nephew for both you and Larkin and set up a time for two days from now. If you remember anything, let me know."

Matthias drew back the curtain, standing for a moment to get his bearings, then heading for the waiting room. He stopped, his eyes closing. If he was here, then his truck wasn't. How was he to get home now?

"Matthias?" He heard a soft voice from beside him and turned, catching his balance as he did so. He stared at the young woman standing here, concern on her face.

"Do I know you?"

She nodded, her shoulder-length curls bobbing with the motion. "I'm Larkin. I want to thank you for saving my life."

"Larkin? I'm sorry. I don't think I know you." Then his words stopped. "You were at the house, weren't you? Are you all right?"

"I am, thanks to you. How are you? Jason said you likely had a concussion."

"No, just a really bad headache. I'd offer you a ride home, but I don't have my truck."

Larkin pointed to the waiting room and he turned. "My brother, Lochlan, is here. We can give you a ride."

Lochlan moved to stand beside his sister, his hand extended to Matthias.

"Thank you, Matthias, for getting Larkin out of the way of that truck."

Matthias shrugged, not really remembering what had transpired. "Not a problem. I hate to ask for a ride."

"Now, that's not a problem at all. Larkin wouldn't leave until she made sure you were okay. Do you live in town?"

Matthias shook his head and then regretted it. "No, I don't. About fifteen minutes towards Oak City."

Lochlan shared a look with his sister. "I would suggest that we take you home with us for the night. Mom will take care of you. I can have your truck brought to our place. I don't think you should be on your own overnight."

Matthias searched Larkin's face and finally nodded. "If it's not too much trouble." He shot a look at Lochlan when he started to laugh.

"No trouble, Matthias. Mom's always taking in waifs and strays." He laughed again at Larkin's soft "Lochlan!". "Wait here. I'll bring my truck around."

Larkin turned to Matthias. "I need to apologize for Lochlan."

Matthias grinned, finally starting to relax. "It's okay. It's not a problem. I've probably said worse to people." He pointed towards the door. "Shall we?"

He stepped back to let Larkin go ahead of him, his eye catching movement to the side. He turned, watching the people around him, fixing his gaze on a man who was standing watching them. He frowned. He didn't know the man, did he? Lord, what now? I'm trying to get away from that life and yet it still hangs on. I have to cling to the hope you give, but it's so hard some days.

Larkin touched his arm, drawing his attention to Lochlan's truck. He held the door for her, then climbed in beside her. What am I letting myself in for, he thought? I really should be on my way home.

He stared out the window, his vision catching a glimpse of the man from the waiting room. Who was he and what did he want?

Matthias finally settled down in the MacTavish's living room, his eyes on

Larkin. She was stretched out on the couch sound, asleep, a tuxedo cat perched on top of her. Matthias smiled as the cat blinked sleepily at him, then reached to wash a paw. He looked around. The house was a home, he thought, something he had never had.

Merry MacTavish watched from the kitchen doorway as her guest had settled down. She walked towards him, coffee mug extended. When he took it was a quiet thanks, she set hers down by her favourite chair, then reached for the throw folded up on the couch, shaking it out and covering her daughter. She settled the cat back down and then sat herself.

Matthias watched her, knowing the love the two women had for one another. He hadn't met Merry's husband, Angus, yet as he was traveling.

"Matthias, you're not from the area. What brought you here?"

"Friends I went to college with. They all settled in this area. I had nothing to take me back to my home area."

"No family?" She watched as he shook his head.

"None. Not for years. I bounced around in foster care since I was 10."

He didn't look up, not wanting to see the pity or condemnation in her face.

She waited, then spoke. "That made it difficult, didn't it? You have triumphed, though, Matthias, shown the naysayers that you are built of better stuff than they thought." His eyes raised, he watched her face. "You're an overcomer, Matthias, in more ways that one. I am pleased and proud to call you a friend. The Lord has certainly blessed you."

Matthias took a moment to absorb what she had said. "He has, Mrs. MacTavish, in many ways. I wouldn't be here but for Him and my last foster family. They were devout Christians and lived what they spoke."

Merry nodded. "It's Merry, please, not Mrs. That's my mother-in-law. I can see their influence. Please, don't be a stranger. We want you as part of our family."

"Even if I bring danger?"

Merry shook her head, her eyes going to Larkin. "Who brought the danger to who,

Matthias? It could easily have been Larkin bringing it to you. Jason will work it through and solve it."

Matthias grinned. "That he will. Now, is there anything I can do for you?"

She shook her head. "I have strict orders that you are to rest today. Lochlan was headed out to get your truck and Larkin's car. Is there something in there that you need?"

He shook his head and pulled out his phone. "I have some reading I can do."

She shook her head. "Sorry, I was not saying you couldn't." She laughed at the expression on his face. "If you want, come with me. I'm going to be working in my gardens and you can help. Just watch for Shamus."

"Shamus?" There's another family member I haven't met, he wondered.

"Yes, Shamus. He's our bi-blue Sheltie and thinks he rules the house. He's been out in the yard. He may be reserved at at first, but once he warms up, you're part of his family."

Larkin stirred, moving slightly and disturbing the cat. Molly gave a disgruntled meow and jumped for the floor, leaving Larkin smiling after her. She sat, brushing her hair back from her face. How long had she slept, she wondered, her eyes narrowed as she looked at the clock. Three hours? She never did that. She rose, padding through the house to the kitchen, grabbing a glass of juice on her way past to the backyard. She stood on the deck, shivers running through her. Someone was watching her, she was sure, but who and where? Her eyes sought the surrounding trees, seeing nothing, then lifted to the houses themselves, not seeing anything there.

Shamus ran towards her, tail wagging, as she stepped outside. She set her glass on the table and swept him into her arms, laughing as he wiggled and licked. Her mother turned from the end of the yard and watched as Larkin headed her way.

"Feeling better, love?"

"I am, Mom. I didn't mean to sleep." She laughed as her mother opened her mouth. "I know what you're going to say. I must have needed it." She turned, eyes watchful. "Where's Matthias?"

"Lochlan and your Dad are here. He's with them in the workshop. Tell me, Larkin. Did you know him before?"

Larkin shook her head. "Not at all. In fact, when he pulled up at that house, I was ready to call 911, I was that scared."

"Good. Not that you're scared of him, but that you were ready to take precautions. And there's nothing in any of your previous cases that would lead to this?"

Larkin stared at her mother. "Mom, why the third degree? You're not the police."

Merry sighed. "I know. I'm just concerned about the two of you."

"It has to have been something with the client. There has to be." Larkin turned and walked away, Shamus running along beside her, nose tilted up to watch her.

She stopped suddenly as she saw boots in her vision and raised her eyes to a laughing face.

"You really need to watch where you're going, you know." Matthias' grin was infectious.

Larkin laughed, her eyes sparkling. "I know. I have a bad habit of that. Dad and Lochlan wear you out with their woodworking?"

"Not at all. My foster father used to do woodworking and taught me lots. I miss it. Whenever I get my house set up the way I would like it, I want to set up a shop."

"That would be good. Dad and Lochlan find it very relaxing." She moved restlessly from foot to foot. "Matthias, can we talk about what happened?"

"Sure. Where would you like to sit?"

"Inside, I think. I feel eyes on me out here."

"You, too?" Her green gaze shot to his. "I've felt it since before I left the hospital. I just pray I didn't bring something your way."

She sat at the kitchen table. "Matthias, what happened this morning? How did we both end up at the wrong house?"

He stared down at his hands, not wanting to face her. When she remained silent, he looked up. "I have no explanation other than we were both given the wrong address. The official take is that the hospital didn't update their records. That's possible, I guess. Who contacted you?"

"Who contacted me? To schedule? I'm not sure. I would have to ask Eve." She reached for her phone. "Eve. Hi! No, I'm better. Just a little accident. We've been able to reschedule? Good. Now about that address? What was that? It was faxed in like usual. What was the fax number it came from? The hospital ward? That's strange. They usually are really good about getting the correct demographics for us. I know. He's going to have fifty million fits. Do me a favour? Lock that referral in the safe. I know. Overkill, but I want it safe. No, I don't think you'll lose it. Okay. I'll see you tomorrow."

She set her phone down in a thoughtful manner before looking at him. "Where did your referral come from, Matthias?"

He thought for a moment. "The hospital ward. And you're right. That is unusual. It usually comes from their client's family physician or specialist office, doesn't it?"

Chapter 3

*L*arkin looked up from her desk as Eve appeared in the doorway the next morning. A frown on her face, she looked at Eve, then down at her paperwork.

"Eve?"

"There's a police detective here to see you, Larkin. A Jason Long."

"Jason? Bring him back, Eve. Thank you." She stood as she waited, pulled her light sweater down over her dress slacks.

"Jason? What brings you by?"

"Larkin. How are you feeling?"

"Better." She moved to close the door, pointing at a chair for Jason. "You're here for a reason."

"I am. It's about yesterday. Go over with me exactly what you did and what happened?"

"Again?"   At his nod, she did so. "And I have to say I felt someone watching me last night at Mom and Dad's. I couldn't see anyone though. Matthias felt the same way."

Jason stopped writing and looked at her. "Have you ever had any issues with clients?"

She shook her head. "None that stand out. Why?"

"Because we need to figure out who was in that truck and why they were there. We also need to figure out who gave you two that address."

She shook her head as she glanced at the clock. "I wish I could help you, Jason, but I can't. I also have to leave to get to a client's house."

He stood, nodding. "If you think of anything at all, no matter how trivial, call me." He handed her a card. "Or Bill. One of us."

She stood staring at the card, a frown on her face. He watched her for a moment.

"Larkin?"

She shook her head, bringing herself back to the present. Looking up, she found his puzzled eyes on her.

"What just happened?"

"I don't know, Jason. Just a feeling, a premonition you would say."

"About what?"

She shrugged. "I have no idea. I'll keep this and call if I have anything." She waved his card in the air.

Matthias stood at his client's door and knocked, a feeling of dread running him. He had never had this feeling before, so why now? What had yesterday been all about? He looked up as the elderly man answered.

"Mr. Black, good to see you up today? How are you feeling?"

The man struggled with his words, but Matthias knew he was speaking better than he had for months.

"I'm just here to do an evaluation today and see what else we can do for you."

The man nodded, then led the way to the kitchen, sitting so Matthias could work. Finally, Matthias stood.

"You're coming along well, Mr. Black. I'm not sure how much further along we'll get your speech but you can certainly make yourself understood."

The man shook his hand, then followed as Matthias walked to the door and left. Matthias stood outside, staring around. Now why did he feel like he was being watched once more? Where was that person?

Matthias watched the truck behind he as he drove back through town. It had followed him now for blocks. He turned towards the library, hoping that the turn would throw the truck off. It seemed to and he sighed as he headed towards the highway and home. It was growing late and after his day yesterday, he just wanted to relax at home.

He pulled into his driveway and stopped, pushing open his door and reaching back for his briefcase. He had paperwork yet to do tonight and he was almost too tired to do it. Walking towards his home, he looked around, once more sure he was being watched. A sudden movement in the dusk came from his left and he found himself on the ground, arm wrestled high behind him, a knee on his back and an arm across his neck. He struggled to rise.

"Where is it?" The guttural voice sounded in his ear.

"Where's what? I don't know what you mean."

"Yes you do. Find it and give it to me. I'll be in touch in twenty-four hours. It would be a shame if anything more happened to that pretty lady." A shove on his back sent his face further into the grass and then the man was gone.

Matthias lay for a few minutes, his breath coming back. Then he dragged himself to his feet, reaching for his briefcase and struggling up his walk to the door. Once inside and the lock fastened behind him, he leaned back, his breath still coming in gasps, his head resting on the door. He had no idea what the man had wanted.

He headed for his office, setting down his briefcase on his desk. Then his hand froze. Someone had been in his office. He spun heading to search the rest of the house. Sighing, he reached for his phone and made the call, the call that would bring the police and detectives and crime scene techs to his home. Just what he needed!

He stood and watched as his home was searched. Running hands through his hair, he finally walked out of the house and starting pacing in his driveway. He saw the officers searching around outside, flashlights illuminating the area. His head turned as he heard footsteps approaching.

"Matthias?"

"Jason? Josiah? What are you two doing here?"

"We heard you had had an incident. Andrew called me and asked me to check on you. Josiah and Faith were having dinner with us."

Matthias nodded as he stared back at his home. "I don't know who it was, Jason, but I think they were following me. A huge black pickup had been on my tail and I thought I had lost him."

"You likely did, but if they're after you, they know where you live. So once again, what were they after?"

"I don't know!" Matthias' voice rose in frustration. "I really don't. I haven't been given anything that I know about. My life is an open book. So who is it and why do they think I have something?"

Jason shared a look with Josiah. "Andrew said something about a time frame."

"Yeah, twenty-four hours to turn it over."

Larkin smiled at the woman sitting in front of her and handed her the remote for her TV.

"Let's see if you can work this today, Mrs. Bell. If you can, then we'll celebrate."

The woman fumbled with it and then pushed the buttons, joy coming to her face when she managed to turn the TV on and to the right channel.

"Thank you, dear." The older woman was recovering from a minor stroke and demanded that she be able to watch her programs. Family couldn't be with her all the time and this helped to pass the time of day for her.

Larkin headed back for her office. It was late and she knew Eve would have gone, but she wanted to get her reports out of the way, that Friday afternoon, and not have anything to hinder her enjoying her weekend. She parked and headed into her office, not heeding the footsteps following her. Unlocking the door, she pushed it open, turning to shove it shut and lock it behind her when it flew open wider, knocking her back into the reception counter. She had a brief glimpse of a man hovering over her, then nothing.

A police cruiser passed through the parking lot a few hours later, stopping at her car. The officer exited and headed for the door, caution in his stance as it opened under his touch. His light caught sight of Larkin on the floor and then as it raised, the tossed look to her office.

Jason strode through the Emergency Department looking for Larkin. He had gotten called that she was there. He sighed. First Matthias and now Larkin. What was the man looking for that he thought one of them had? He spoke with the Emergency Physician, and then ducked behind one of the curtains. Larkin lay on the stretcher, eyes closed, bruising evident on her face. One arm was wrapped.

Jason stood for a moment, then turned. He would be back. Word had come that she was being admitted overnight. This is going to play havoc with her schedule, he thought. Thankfully it was Friday and she had a couple of days to recuperate.

Matthias stood as Jason appeared in the waiting room and walked towards him.

"Matthias?   What are you doing here?"

"Lochlan called me. How is she?"

"She was sleeping. I'll have to come back." Jason looked around, then pointed at chairs in the corner. "Let's sit."

"What do you want to know, Jason? I know that look of yours."

Jason stared around the room. "There has to be something, Matthias. Why you two? You're not connected, had never met.

She's from here. You're not. What do they think you have?"

Matthias shrugged. "I have no idea, Jason, and I doubt Larkin does either. I haven't received anything or seen anything that I shouldn't have."

"I get that, Matthias. I need to talk to Larkin too." He sighed. "There are times when I wish I had chosen another occupation."

"Why? You're good at what you do."

"I know. I just had seeing friends hurt. Somehow I don't think this is going to get any easy for either one of you. It never does."

Chapter 4

Larkin moved her head, her eyes sliding open and closed. She didn't have a clue where she was, but it certainly wasn't her own bed. Her eyes opened again and stayed open for her to stare around. She sighed. I'm in the hospital and I have no idea why. The last I remember is walking towards my office. She turned as she heard movement near her.

"Lochlan? What are you doing here?"

Her brother roused and then stood at her bedside. "How are you feeling?"

She shrugged, her movements careful. "I've got a brutal headache. What happened?"

"You were attacked at your office last night. Do you remember anything at all?"

She shook her head, regretting it as she grimaced with pain. "Nothing."

Lochlan pushed the call button. "The nurse asked if I would let them know when you woke. They want to assess you and then give you some pain medications."

She shook her head. "No, Lochlan. I don't want that. They'll give me something really strong. What else is going on? You're holding something back."

He sighed, his eyes going towards the window hidden by the curtain, then back to her, the colour matching her own, his hair just a shade lighter than hers. "Matthias was attacked the other night, too, and his home ransacked. Your office was as well. Jason had Eve come in this morning and go over what was there. They didn't find anything out of the ordinary."

"How long have I been here?"

"It's Saturday, Larkin. You've been sleeping on and off for the last eighteen hours. The doctors said you had a concussion which explained that."

She laid her head back, groaning. "Lochlan, I have clients to see Monday. I need out of here."

"We know that, Larkin. We're trying to figure out how to keep you safe."

She pointed at him. "Out. I'm getting dressed and leaving."

"No, Larkin. You need to stay."

She just gave him that look and he threw up his hands.

"All right. I'll wait for you, but don't expect it to go over well with the hospital."

Larkin walked slowly down the hospital corridor, her head pounding. Maybe Lochlan was right, she should have stayed, but she wouldn't give him the satisfaction of hearing her admit that. She stopped as she saw boots in her line of sight. Moving her eyes upwards, she met Matthias' concerned gaze.

"Larkin? I thought they weren't going to release you yet."

She snorted. "Like I would stay here? What are you doing here? And how are you anyway?"

"I'm fine. I came to see you." He reached out a hand to steady her as he watched the nurse come up behind her with a wheelchair. "Here, you need to sit before you fall down."

"I'm not leaving here in a wheelchair."

"And I say you are. If you don't, I'll turn you right around and take you back to that room you just came from and tie you down to make you stay." Matthias' face hid his real feelings, that she was hurt worse that they thought.

She gave him her best glare without effect. Then, she sighed.

"All right, if that's what it takes to get me out of here. You're driving me home right?"

"To your parents."

She shook her head. "No, my home. I need to go there."

He looked past her at Lochlan, who shook his head as he stood waiting for Larkin to approach his truck.

"Matthias, will you take me home? Lochlan will smother me if he does."

Matthias shot her brother a look, then looked down at her. Lord, what's going on here? I feel like I've walked right into something.

Mathias approached Lochlan and after a few minutes of conversation, went for his truck. Lochlan slowly approached his sister, eyes trying to read her mood

"Larkin?"

"I know, Lochlan. You want to protect me, but you smother me. Just humour me this time, okay?"

He shrugged, eyes worried. This was not Larkin.

Matthias pulled away from the hospital entrance and turned to Larkin.

"You'll have to direct me."

She slowly nodded, hand on her head. "First, Matthias, I need to stop at the office. I want to pack up my things and move them home. Whoever is after me, if he keeps going after me, I'm putting everyone else there at risk."

"Are you sure?" At her small nod, he turned for her office. "Do you have a lot and do you need boxes?"

"We have enough boxes stored away I should be okay. I don't have a lot as most of my records are digital."

Matthias shoved the last box into the bed of his truck, then turned to head back into the office. His steps stopped and he glanced around. *There it is again, Lord, that feeling of evil. Who is it?* He reached to steady Larkin as she headed towards him.

"Let's get you sitting down, Larkin. You'll have to direct me to your place."

"It's not far, just on the outskirts of town. Those boxes can go into my office for now." She sighed. "I'll need to pick up a filing cabinet."

"I can do that for you. In fact, I have a brand new one at home that I've never used. It's not too far. Let me head that way and get it."

"I can't let you do that." Larkin turned in surprise to him.

"You're not. I offered."

Later that afternoon, Matthias stopped to watch Larkin as she sat as her desk, laptop open in front of her.

"You need to rest, Larkin. Here's your peppermint tea."

"Thank you. I'm done." She sighed. "I just need to find someone to drive me around Monday."

"Your Mom?" When she shook her head, he continued, "You know Zeke and Paige Williams?" When she looked up and nodded, he added, "Paige has called. She'll drive you on Monday. She doesn't have clients she needs to see in the office."

"Why?"

"Why what?"

Larkin turned to look at Matthias. "Why would she do that for me?"

"Because that's who she is. She gives and doesn't expect it back. She and Zeke went through some really hard stuff a while ago and that made her want to help others."

Larkin finally shrugged. "Okay, then. Tomorrow, I'll rest and be ready for Monday."

Matthias stared at her. "You're staying by yourself tonight?"

She nodded. "Of course, I am. I'm not going to Mom's."

Matthias shook his head. "Not a good idea, Larkin. You've just come out of the hospital and have a concussion to boot."

She stared at him. "What would you have me do?"

He ran his hands through his hair, then pointed at the door. "I'll be right outside, in my truck, and I'll be checking on you every two hours. Let me have your phone number." When she went to protest, he continued, "It's that, or I pack you up and take you to your Mom's. Which will it be?"

She kept staring at him. "You can't be serious! You're worse than Lochlan!"

"And Lochlan says he'll be sleeping on your couch tonight." Matthias watched the emotions racing across her face. "Larkin, we have no idea who this is or what they want. We've both been attacked. Now what will it be?"

She turned to walk away, staggering slightly. Matthias' hands came out to steady her. Tears in her eyes, she finally nodded.

"Your way. Just go now, Matthias. I need some time."

Lochlan approached Matthias as he stood, back leaning against his truck, eyes on the front door.

"She's not going along with your plan?" Lochlan was prepared to go and pack a bag for his sister.

"She did." Lochlan shot him a glance. "She's not happy, but she agreed. She asked for a couple of hours or so."

"How did you get her to agree? I would have said she wouldn't."

"Prayer, Lochlan. Lots of prayer." He turned to study the street around him. "Tell me something. When did your sister lose her hope?"

"Lose her hope? Whatever are you talking about?" Lochlan stared at him.

"She's hurting, Lochlan. Way deep inside. She's hiding it, but I've been where she's at. She needs to find that hope in God once more."

Lochlan leaned his arms on Matthias' truck and laid his head down on them. "I had no idea. We're twins, you know. She's older by a few minutes. We're supposed to have this connection, aren't we? Aren't we supposed to know how the other feels?"

"They say that, but I have no idea, Lochlan. I have no siblings, so I wouldn't know."

Chapter 5

Matthias stood in his backyard a week later, his thoughts playing back over the week. He hadn't seen Larkin but had talked to her a couple of times on the phone. That wasn't enough for him. He wanted to see her face to face, to see what she was hiding. Lord, what's she hiding and how can I help? He lost himself in his prayer, not hearing the singing of the spring birds, the sound of the breeze through the opening leaves. He didn't see the spring flowers cropping up around his yard. All he saw was Larkin's face and the hurt she had deep in her eyes.

He turned, determination in his steps, pulling out his phone as it rang. He stopped, surprise on his face.

"Larkin? Hi!"

"Are you busy, Matthias? I'm sorry, I shouldn't have called."

"Larkin? What's going on?"

"I need to talk to someone, and I don't want to call Mom or Dad, and Lochlan would have my head."

"Larkin, what did you do?" Matthias pulled his keys out even as he ran for his truck.

"I don't know, Matthias. I just found something in my paperwork, and I don't think it's mine. Oh, what have I done?"

"Larkin, stay on the phone with me. I'm on my way. Ten minutes max."

"Matthias! You'll get a ticket, and that will be my fault." He could hear tears in her voice.

"No, I won't. Talk to me, hon. What's going on?"

"I can't explain it over the phone. I need you to see it." Her voice went silent. "Or maybe I should just call Jason."

"Larkin, I'm at your door. Open it for me, hon." He reached for her as soon as she pulled the door open, sweeping her into a hug.

Her arms tight around him, she shook, the shudders making Matthias almost weep.

"Larkin, what is it?"

She stepped back, and grabbing his hand, pulled her with him almost on a run to her office, pointing at the paperwork she had spread around the floor. "There! I have no idea what that means. It's not mine! Where did I get it?"

"What is it?" He shot a quick look at the papers, then fastened his gaze on her. His hands on her cheeks, he made her look at him, his heart sinking as he saw the look in her eyes. "Larkin, sit! I'll be right back."

Matthias handed her the bottle of water he found in her fridge. When she didn't take it, he sighed, opened it, and closed her fingers around it

"Drink, Larkin. You need to."

She finally did, her eyes not leaving the floor.

"Now, what did you find?"

She raised her eyes to his. "Take a look at the paperwork on top. I have no idea whose it's supposed to be."

He picked it up, read it, and then sat beside her. "Okay, so we back track a bit.

How long have you been in that office suite?"

She shrugged. "Four years, maybe? There are seven of us in it, including Eve. She's the receptionist for us all, handles the faxing, the appointment requests. We book our own appointments, do our own billing, our own paperwork." She stabbed a finger at what he held. "That's why I have no idea how I got that."

He studied it again. "I think we need to talk to Jason at least, if not Bill. This is likely what the man was searching for. But why he came after me, I have no idea. I've never seen this before."

He leafed through the pages again, finally stopping at the second last one. "Did you notice this, Larkin?"

"Notice what?" She leaned against his arm to study the paper, and he got a whiff of coconut from her hair. "Oh, my! Wasn't that the client we were supposed to see? That's the address."

"It is. I don't like this." He reached for his phone, then looked at the time. "Jason and Maria are away until tomorrow. I don't like to leave this. Let me try Bill."

"Bill? Hi. No, I'm fine now. Listen, are you on call this weekend? You are? Terrific. You heard what happened to Larkin and I, I suspect. I'm at her place. She found some paperwork that's not hers. Can you drop by? That's her address. Supper? I guess it would be okay. See you in a bit."

An hour later, Larkin sat back, dropping her piece of pizza on her plate. Bill had the paperwork laid out in front of him, studying it.

"You've never seen it before, Larkin?" When she shook her head, he frowned. "It doesn't have a name on it for one of your coworkers either, but it has your fax number. Do each of you have your own fax number?"

"We do. I've had mine changed to come in here to the house. I've given up my office at the building."

"Tell me how it worked. Each one with their own fax machine and who had access to it?"

"Each had one. The only ones who had access to them was the worker and Eve. She would just sort through the faxes and put them into appointments or other faxes. Now, I have it set up to have the faxes come right into the computer."

"Is that what he was looking for, Bill?" Matthias finally spoke.

Bill shrugged. "It could be. By itself, it really doesn't say much, other than it's a property listing for that house you were at. Unless…." Bill's voice dropped off. "Let me work in this. I have an idea."

"Sure. Just let us know what you find out." Matthias shared a look with Larkin

"I will. I need to run. Stay safe, you two."

Larkin stood to clear the table, turning at Matthias returned. "We're no further ahead, are we?"

Matthias shrugged. "Doesn't really look like it, does it"

"Will that guy come back?" Matthias heard the fear in her voice. He approached her, hands on her shoulders.

"I don't know, Larkin. He might. If he thinks we still have what he wants." He stared at the wall in front of him, not seeing anything. "I don't like that you're here alone."

Larkin pushed away from him. "I'm not moving from my house, Matthias. Not a chance."

He nodded, his eyes on her face. "Now, about tomorrow. Do you have plans?"

She shook her head, eyes apprehensive. "Why?"

"Nothing bad, Larkin. Let me take you to church and then out for dinner."

She choked back a retort, studying him. "Church and dinner? I don't know, Matthias."

"Please?"

He saw the struggle she was going through, and then the moment she gave in. A slight smile on his face, he waited for her answer.

"All right. Whose church?"

"It doesn't matter. I just want to spend the time with you."

"All right. My church. It's not fancy, Matthias. I usually just go in jeans and a sweater or nice top."

"That's good to know. Mine's more formal. I think I like the sound of yours." He stopped at the door. "Do you have an alarm system?" At her nod, he continued, "Make sure it's set tonight. I'll see you in the morning."

Larkin watched him walk away, seeing how he looked around. She shivered, arms crossed in front of her. He's out there, isn't he? Please, Lord, remove him from here. I need to feel safe and I don't, not any more

Chapter 6

*M*atthias drew a breath of relief as he sat beside Larkin the next morning. He had expected her to call him and cancel. He looked around her church and then to the front, noting the simplicity of the building but the rugged cross on the dais. He turned as she touched his arm.

"Are you okay?" Her eyes showed her concern.

"I am, Larkin. Thank you for asking. This is just so different."

She grinned at him. "Not what you were expecting, was it?"

"Not at all." He lifted what he would call a bulletin, not quite sure what she called it. "This is nice. I like how it's laid out. I also like that your pastor gives you an insert to take notes."

"That is nice, isn't it? He's been working through some pretty heavy stuff lately, laying it on the line. He's working through hope and what that means right now. I thought one sermon and that would be it. Nope. He's on his fifth one already."

"Five? Wow! He really must be mining the scriptures."

"He does. What he says is from the Bible and very challenging."

Standing at the end of the service, Matthias looked around, suddenly uncomfortable. He waited for Larkin to move out ahead of him, then walked beside her, his hand on her back. She stopped to greet friends and introduce him. Finally, he thought, they were out of the crowd and walking towards his truck.

"Where to now, Matthias?" She grinned up at him. "You did promise me lunch."

"I did, didn't I?" He helped her into the truck, then moved quickly to slid behind the wheel. "How hungry are you?"

She shrugged. "I always have a good appetite. Why?"

"Because there's a little restaurant about thirty minutes from here I'd like to take you to. It's very unique."

"I guess, if I have to, I can wait that long."

Matthias shot her a glance, saw the sparkle of mischief in her eyes, and started laughing. "Hmm. I know of another nice one that's an hour away."

"No. I think the first one will do."

Matthias watched his mirrors as he drove. He had the feeling he was being followed but couldn't see a vehicle stand out.

Larkin stood beside Matthias, staring at the building. "Really, Matthias? This can't be a restaurant!"

He laughed as he took her hand. "It is, Larkin. It used to be a one-room school house and the present owner's parents bought it and converted it. Come on."

He held the door for her, almost walking into her as she stopped. Hands on her shoulders, he moved her off to the side so she could look around.

"This is amazing! I like how they kept so much of the school room feel. Those desks and blackboards. The floor. Even the old stove in the corner."

He grinned. "It is cool, isn't it? Come on. My favourite table's still empty."

She stared at the menu, intrigued by the names of the meals. "Where did they come up with these?"

Matthias started laughing. "The present owner's Mom was a school teacher. These are her creations."

"I like them"

Matthias's gaze rose from her face as the door opened and two men entered. He shuddered, the evil emanating from them felt across the room.

"Matthias?" Larkin's voice caught his attention. "Are you okay?"

He sighed to himself. "Yeah, I'm fine." He drew from within himself to smile at her. "What did you decide to have?"

"I think the History platter - it sounds intriguing with the array of meats."

"It is good. I'm going to have the Spelling burger."

She started to giggle. "Spelling burger? How many letters are in it?"

He laughed with her. "Just wait. You'll want to come back here more than once."

Larkin settled back into the truck seat, smiling as Matthias slid behind the wheel. "Thank you, Matthias. This has been wonderful."

"You're welcome. I'll bring you again some time and you can sample another subject."

She laughed, then pointed at his windshield. "What's that under the wiper blade?"

Matthias stared at it, then stepped from the truck, reaching for the piece of paper. He read it, his fear and anger growing. They were threatening both Larkin and himself, whoever they were. They had been here. His feeling of being followed had been right.

He climbed back into the truck, his face emotionless.

"Matthias?"

He stared through the windshield for a few moments before handing her the note. She took it, her eyes not leaving his face.

"They followed up, Larkin. How I don't know, but they were in the restaurant with us."

"Matthias! Who are they?"

He shook his head. "They've threatened you, Larkin." He turned his eyes to her. "They've threatened you and I don't know how to stop them."

She looked from him to the note and then back at him. "How?"

He pointed at the note. "Read it. We need to talk to Bill or Jason today."

She looked down, her eyes following the words. "Matthias, are they serious?"

"I would say they are."

She read aloud: *"Bring us the information you found or you die. Twenty-four hours."*

"We don't have that paperwork." She looked up at him, fear in her eyes.

"I know we don't. What I want to know is how they knew you had it."

"Eve. It has to have been Eve. She must to have seen it and said something to someone. I didn't see it until just before I showed it to you."

"I know." He pulled out his phone and tossed her to her. "You'll find Bill's number in my contacts. Call him. Let him know we're heading his way." He reached for her hand and squeezed it. "I didn't mean for our meal out together to end like this."

"It's not your doing, Mathias. I just wish I knew who this was."

Bill studied the two sitting in front of his desk, then looked down at the paper.

"You found it on your windshield? No one around?"

Matthias shook his head. "No one, although there were a couple of men who came into the restaurant after us. I felt really uncomfortable about them."

"Can you describe them?"

Matthias shook his head. "Not really, other than they were dark haired and stocky, definitely less than six feet in height."

Larkin watched him in surprise. "I didn't see them."

"No. Your back was to them and you were having too much fun reading the menu."

Bill shot a glance between the two. Okay, Lord, so what's going on with these two? And please, not again.

"That's pretty general, Matthias. If you think of anything else about them, let me know."

"Those papers, Bill? What about them?" Larkin's question had Bill sitting back down.

"Those papers! They were interesting to say the least. I showed them to Andrew. He's never seen anything like them before. And Eve is avoiding my calls. I even drove by her apartment, but she wasn't home."

Larkin frowned. "That's not Eve, Bill. She never doesn't answer, and I know she never goes out anywhere on Sunday. Can you take me by her place? I have a key to get in. I've fed her fish for her when she's been away."

"Sure. Let's go."

Bill stood at Eve's door as Larkin knocked, then opened it with her key.

"Stay out here with Matthias, Larkin. I'm going in to search."

Bill entered, his eyes searching in the darkness. He stopped as he approached the kitchen, seeing bare feet on the floor. He reached around to feel for a pulse, and then stood, backing away and out the door, his phone out to make a call.

Matthias and Larkin looked at him. Then Larkin started to the door, stopping when Matthias wrapped his arms around her from behind.

"It's too late for Eve, Larkin. Come, let's get out of Bill's way. We'll go wait downstairs." He nodded as he caught Bill's look.

"But, is she home? Bill? Is Eve all right?"

Bill turned, a sad look on his face. "I'm sorry, Larkin. Eve's dead."

Hands to her mouth, Larkin staggered, only kept upright by Matthias' arm. "No! That can't be!"

"I'm sorry.   Let Matthias take you back to your place. I'll come find you when I'm done."

Chapter 7

_L_arkin paced her living room, arms wrapped around her waist.   Shock was setting in and the tears she had been trying to hold back fell, streaking down her cheeks. Matthias gave a soft sigh and then went to her, wrapping her tight in his arms.   She clung to him as she sobbed.

"Why, Matthias?   Why did this happen? Where's God in this?"

His head on hers, Matthias said nothing, just prayed for her. He finally felt her body sag and when he looked down, she was asleep. He gathered her up and sat on the couch, dragging the afghan around her. How long, Lord, will this go on and how hurt will she be?   I don't know if I can handle another friend going through this.

He looked up as a tap came at the door and then it cracked open. Bill stood at the living room entrance, then entered and sat, a sigh echoing around the room. He was exhausted. He didn't know if he had the heart to go through more of this.

"Bill?"

"Matthias, how long has Larkin been sleeping?"

"A couple of hours, I think. Do you need her away?"

Bill shook his head. "Not necessarily. I can talk to her tomorrow."

"Can you say anything?" Matthias watched as Bill scrubbed a hand down his face.

"Not a whole lot right now. She was strangled, the ME thinks sometime Friday night. We're trying to track her last movements, but she really didn't have many friends or go many places other than home and work."

"That's so sad, Bill." Matthias looked down as Larkin stirred, then sat up, pushing the hair from her face.

She frowned as she stared at Bill. "What are you doing here?"

Bill grinned and waited.

"All right, spill. What did you find out?"

"Larkin!" Matthias' shocked voice broke through the silence that followed.

"What? He knows something. He can tell us." She glared at him.

"All right, you two. I was just telling Matthias that Eve was killed sometime on Friday evening. We're trying to trace her movements."

"Friday evening? She always picked up an Italian dinner and took it home. She had a stack of movies she watched over and over. That was her release from work." Larkin stared at Bill. "How did she die?"

"Strangled."

"Oh, yuck! That's a horrible way to die!"

Matthias had to struggle to choke back laughter at the expression on her face. The situation wasn't funny, but her reaction was just so Larkin.

"Now what, Bill? She can't tell us about that paperwork, so where do we go from here?"

"We don't go anywhere, Larkin. I do as does my team. You two stay out of it!"

She snorted, bring laughter from the two men. "Not highly likely, Bill. They've threatened my life. I'll be after them."

"Larkin, listen to me. You need to let us do our job. Part of that is keeping you safe. We can't do that if you get mixed up in this."

"We already are, Bill." She stood and paced to the kitchen, returning with a glass of juice. "If it wasn't for us, you wouldn't have an investigation.

Matthias snickered, drawing a glare from Bill. "She's right, you know. I think we caused this."

Bill shook his head. "No, you two didn't. Whoever is behind it did. What can I say to make you two stay out of the investigation?"

"I don't think there's much you can, Bill. Larkin is going to want to be involved, and it will take all my effort to keep her out of it."

Larkin stared at Matthias. "Who says you're going to keep me out of it?"

"I do!" The men spoke in unison, staring her down, or rather trying to.

She stared back at them. "Not highly likely. Now if you gentlemen will excuse me, it's time you two left. I have to work in the morning and I need my sleep."

The men left, Matthias stopping to have a quiet word with her.

"Do you really think she'll stay out of it, Bill?"

He shook his head. "Unfortunately, I don't think she will. Talk some sense into her, please."

Matthias stared in the distance, jiggling his truck keys in his hand. "Somehow, Bill, I don't think anything we say will work. And I don't think those men are finished. They gave her twenty-four hours to produce that paperwork you have. What do we do about that?"

"Let me think on it and I'll call you in the morning." He turned to look back at the house. "She's running scared, Matthias. She has been for years. I talked to her parents yesterday. They've tried to find out what's wrong and haven't been able to."

"She's a very private person, Bill. Until the right person asks the right questions, she won't talk."

"Let's pray that you're that person, Matthias. She's too fragile, even though she seems not to be."

"I know. This bit isn't helping. I sense that she really doesn't have a lot of hope in her life, despite what she says."

Larkin locked her door behind her the next night, more exhausted than she thought she could be. She dropped her briefcase on her desk and then sat. She had paperwork to do, but it could wait for a while. She leant back, eyes thoughtful. It was now more than twenty-four hours since she had been given the ultimatum. When would those men appear next?

As her doorbell sounded, she jumped, fear then freezing her for a moment. Then she moved to peek out the door, finally opening it.

"Edie, what are you doing here?" She drew the older woman into the house, shutting the door.

"Bringing you these!"   Edie Snow held up a bouquet of yellow roses.

"For me?"   At her nod, Larkin took them and headed for the living room.   "Sit. Edie, who are these from?"

"Check the card.   But first, let me tell you.   If I was your age, and a tall good-looking man entered my life and I was single, I wouldn't let him get away."   Edie laughed at Larkin's expression.   "So, this is how it went.   A young man walks into my store today, up to the counter, and tells me he knows you used to work for me.   Asks me what your favourite flower is and then picks out that vase."

Larkin stared at Edie, mouth slightly open.   "No way!"

"Yes, way!   Listen, Larkin.   I know you don't trust men easily and I don't know why.   This young man seems to think the world of you.   I don't know him so I hope he's all right."   At Larkin's nod, she stood. "I'm going to make us some tea.   It's been a good while since we talked.   We have some catching up to do."

Edie walked towards the kitchen as Larkin watched.   Larkin reached for the envelope with the card, studying the strong handwriting of her name. She pulled out the card, stopping to read it, her cheeks going pink with a blush. Edie was watching from the kitchen doorway and nodded. Lord, let him be the one.

Larkin traced the handwriting with her finger. *"Larkin, just to say thanks for being who you are. I'm glad you're in my life. Matthias. Xoxo"*

Now, Larkin thought to herself, did he really mean those two letters at the end? Her gaze fastened once more on the roses and she touched the petals.

Edie stood watching, cups of tea in hand.

"He's worth it, Larkin. Whatever it is that's in your past, leave it there. Get to know this young man. Now, tell me what's up with you?"

"Edie, you've lived here all your life and know most of the people in town. What can you tell me about Alice Taylor?"

"Alice? My word, girl, why do you ask? She must be over 80 now, if she's a day. I know she used to live out on the farm, until she had to move to town. That property is just sitting there, waiting for her to die. Then it goes to the next in line. There's a clause in the will that says it can't be sold, it has to be passed down to family. This goes way back."

"That's interesting. I didn't know they still did that."

"Once in a while, that happens. Listen, I need to run. I promised your young man I would hand deliver those. Now, don't be a stranger." With a hug, Edie was gone.

Larkin locked the door after her, then stopped in front of the roses, a softened look on her face as she once more touched the petals. She reached for the card, reading it over and wondering just what Matthias had meant. She sighed. Nothing more than friend, she thought. She wasn't the type to have a boyfriend, let alone a husband.

She reached for her phone, pulling up his number in her contacts, hesitating before she dialed.

Listening to his voice mail greeting, she was torn about leaving a message.

"Matthias, hi. It's Larkin. I just wanted to say thank you for the roses. That was so sweet of you."

Matthias listened to her voice as she left the message, a smile on his face. There was something about her that drew him to her. He turned at the knock at his door.

"Bill? What are you doing here?" He stepped back to let Bill enter, Andrew, the acting town police chief on loan from the county with him. "Sit. Can I get you anything? I just put on a pot of coffee."

"That sounds good, Matthias." Andrew pulled back a chair and sank down at the kitchen table, relieved to be off his feet.

"Bad day, Andrew?" Matthias set the mug in front of him and reached the tin of cookies.

"They all seem to be lately, Matthias." Andrew stared at his friend, then down at his mug. "Tell me what's going on with you and Larkin?"

"Larkin? Nothing. Why?"

Andrew's face broke into a smile. "That's not what I'm hearing. Church, lunch, flowers."

Matthias stared at him, finally catching the sparkle of mischief in his eyes. Shaking his head, he spoke, "You'll be the last to know. Now, why are you here?"

Andrew swallowed the mouthful of coffee and then nodded. "It's about that property and those papers. You're not from here, so you wouldn't know the family."

"What about them?"

"First, the property - it can never be sold, not matter who inherits it. There have been rumours for years of mineral rights being sought, but they can't be signed away at all. Secondly, the lady who owns the house now hasn't lived there for a number of years. She moved into town to an apartment when her husband died."

"So who inherits?" Bill spoke, not quite sure any more who the family was.

"That's the thing. She's the last of the family. When she dies, the property goes into a trust and can't even be sold then. From what I understand, there is money set aside to repair the house and property and it will become something for charity."

"Wow!" Matthias sat back in his chair. "So why were we run down?"

"That's what we don't get either. We're still working on that."

Matthias shook his head as he stared at his two friends. "I really don't get it. We weren't out there for anything other than a patient. And who gave us that wrong information? Is there a clause if someone dies or is seriously hurt on the property that something can then be done?"

Andrew and Bill shared a look, the thought never having crossed their mind.

"That's an interesting question, Matthias. I'll have to look into that." Bill stood. "Listen I have to run. Catch you later."

Andrew watched Matthias for a few moments, then spoke. "How serious is it with Larkin?"

Matthias looked up, expecting Andrew to be teasing him. He took in the solemn look on his friend's face. "What do you mean?"

"Just what I asked. How serious are you?"

Matthias shrugged. "I want to get to know her better, but she's a hard read."

Andrew nodded. "She always has been, Matthias. I don't know why. Lochlan can't explain it either. Edie Snow has tried for years to get her to open up to her and she has."

"Edie Snow? As in Edie the florist?"

Andrew grinned as he nodded. "I bet you went there for flowers, didn't you? And Edie promised to hand deliver them? That's Edie. Larkin worked for her during high school and college. At one point, we thought she would go into partnership with Edie."

"Why didn't she?"

Andrew frowned. "We have no idea. We think something happened at some point with a customer or sales agent, but Larkin never said. And if Edie knows, she's not saying either." Shooting a quick glance at the clock, Andrew stood. "I'm out of here as well. Listen, about Larkin. Just be her friend. Let her know you're there even if she tries to drive you away. And she will try that, I guarantee you."

"Thanks, Andrew. Keep me updated will you?"

Matthias stood on the front steps, looking around after Andrew drove away. He could feel it, the thought. That evil out there.

Chapter 8

Larkin turned in a circle in her backyard, feeling eyes on her. Where is he, Lord? I'm getting tired of this, of feeling like I'm being watched, of being scared, of not being able to be myself with my friends. She headed for her house, then stopped. What was that package on her patio?

Standing over it, she read her name in bold black letters. No return address, she thought. I don't like this. Who would do this? And why the back door, not the front door? Sighed, she headed into the house, looking for her phone.

"Hi, Bill. Are you on duty tonight? Good. I have a package on my back patio. No, just my name. I'm not expecting anything. No, I don't think Matthias has sent me anything else. Would you stop! Okay, see you in five. No way am I going back out there. How did they get back there? That's what I would like to know. I keep the gate locked and it's a high fence."

Matthias stood behind the police lines, watching as the bomb squad headed to the back of Larkin's home, Lochlan beside him.

"What's going on, Matthias?" Lochlan's voice was tight with worry.

"I don't know, Lochlan. I just got here." Matthias watched at Bill walked Larkin towards them.

"Larkin?" Lochlan reached to hug his sister, then dropped his arms when she moved away to stand by Matthias. He watched, a look of curiosity on his face.

"Larkin?" Matthias tilted his head to look into her face.

Larkin gave him one look and then reached to hug him, his arms wrapping around her in surprise. "I found a package on my patio. We're not sure yet what it is."

"A package?" Matthias' eyes shot to Bill and then to Lochlan.

Bill nodded. "Just her name, nothing else. The bomb squad will check it out first for us. Then we'll have the crime scene team move in.   Who'd you make as an enemy, Larkin?"

She shook her head, face still buried against Matthias. "No one that I know of, Bill. At least not for years."

"Care to clarify that?"

She sighed, finally turning to face him, still safe in Matthias' arms. "I'll talk when we're somewhere more quiet and safer."

They watched as the bomb squad leader approached, a grim look on his face.

"Who'd you make angry, Larkin?" He lifted his helmet from his head.

"What do you mean?"

"That was a pretty sophisticated bomb, not made by an amateur.   Who'd you anger?"

Larkin shook her head, tremors running through her body. "No one that I know of."

"Whoever it is knows what they're doing, or who to hire." He handed Bill an envelope. "We didn't open this. It was just inside the box. If Larkin had opened the box and lifted the letter, she would be gone. I would say someone knew her well enough to know she'd call for help before she moved the package." He turned and walked back to his squad.

Bill looked at the letter, then at Larkin. "Okay, Larkin. Let's head to the department. Lochlan, she's safe now. If you want to come you can. Matthias, get your lady in your truck and downtown."

Larkin sank back against Matthias. "Bill?"

"Move it, Larkin. Whoever sent you the package is here somewhere watching. We need to get you out of sight."

Larkin stared at Bill, then moved as Matthias pulled her with him to his truck. Lochlan stopped for a word with Bill, then followed as they headed downtown.

Bill tucked the three into a boardroom and then went looking for Andrew.

"Andrew, got a few moments?"

Andrew looked up at Bill, then sat back in his chair. "What's up?"

"Larkin had a bomb placed on her patio tonight. Don't worry, it didn't go off.

But this letter was inside it.   It's just so strange."

"What did the letter say?"

"I haven't opened it yet." Bill held up the evidence bag. "I didn't want to open it in front of Larkin."

Bill pulled back the envelope flap and pulled out the letter, his gloved hands feeling clumsy.   He opened the letter, a frown gathering on his face. He looked up at Andrew.

"This is strange, Andrew."

"What do you mean?" He reached for the letter Bill handed him.

Andrew scanned it, then went back and read it over more slowly. "You're right, Bill. It is strange."

Andre laid the letter down and studied it once more.

"You lose. Time is running out. Give us what we want and you may live. Tick. Tock."

"How does this work in with the other threats?" Bill asked.

"That I have no clue." Andrew stood, dropping the letter into an evidence bag. He turned the envelope over and then put it into its own bag.

They walked into the boardroom, Larkin and Matthias turning to watch them, Lochlan watching from his post against the far wall.

"Bill? Andrew? I don't like that look on your faces." Larkin's eyes traced between the two men.

"We don't either, Larkin. Now, tell me. Who'd you tick off so badly they set a bomb at your place?" Andrew watched her intently.

Larkin sat back in her chair, unsure of what he meant. "No one, Andrew. I don't have enemies."

"No enemies, Larkin? Yet someone tried to run you two down, searched your office, knocking you out in the process, and now sets a bomb on your patio. Someone's trying to tell you something."

Larkin shook her head. "I have no idea, Andrew. You have to believe me."

"Anything in your past we should know about? You said something at your house."

Larkin sighed, then dropped her head to her arms folded on the table. Matthias' hand went to her back and rubbed it. She finally lifted her head, her eyes meeting her brother.

"Lochlan, do you remember when I worked for Edie?" At his nod, she continued. "A sales rep for one of the suppliers always tried to get me to go out with him. Edie never knew. He always asked when we were alone. The last time I refused, he grew somewhat aggressive. Edie walked in on that and sent him packing. She complained to his company and he actually lost his job. But I don't think he would wait all these years to get back at me."

"Not likely. Let us have his name and we'll check him out. No one else?"

Larkin gave it to him and then turned to Matthias. "But he wasn't from the area, so how did he know about you? The only way someone would get both of us out there is if the referral was directed by either the hospital or her family physician. That's how my referrals come."

"Mine, too." Matthias shared a look with Lochlan before looking at Bill and Andrew. "I'm going to trace back where the referral came from. I think Larkin needs to do the same. And before you ask, because of patient confidentiality, neither one of you can. We'll let you know what we find out."

Bill nodded. "I don't have to remind you to that you need to be very careful. Whoever this is plays for keeps."

Larkin shuddered at the thought. "Do you know how he got into my backyard?"

"Picked the lock. I would suggest you go to a different lock, Larkin. Both of you need to make sure your alarm system is a good one and working well."

Lochlan watched the look on his sister's face, knowing how she felt about alarms. "You need to do this, Larkin. We need to keep you safe."

She stared at him, then nodded finally. "I know. I just hate all this." She looked at the two officers. "Are we done? Can I go home?"

Bill and Andrew shared a look before Andrew spoke. "Just be very careful. You as well, Matthias." Andrew stood, his gaze on the two, and then on Lochlan. He frowned as he caught the look on Lochlan's face, then smiled to himself. Yeah, you see it too, don't you, Lochlan? They do make a cute couple.

Larkin finally stood, her eyes on her brother. "Lochlan, I can see you're thinking. What is it?"

Lochlan sighed as he shoved away from the wall and rounded the table to his sister. He drew her into a hug, his chin on her head.

"I'm just trying to think of who it would be, Larkin. We grew up in this town. It's small. You would think we would know who's evil."

"You would think that, but evil can hide. You know what the Bible says, a wolf in sheep's clothing. Maybe what we need to do is research the land surrounding that place. Maybe that's what the issue is."

Lochlan stood for a moment, then stepped back, hands on her shoulders. "You just made me remember something. About ten years ago, I heard rumours of underground wealth but no one ever confirmed it or denied. Let me see what I can come up with."

"Just be careful, Lochlan. Whoever these people are, they seem to be getting more and more violent." Her eyes searched the eyes that matched hers in colour.

"I will, Larkin. I don't need to tell you to be careful either. Matthias, take care of her, please." Dropping a kiss on her cheek, Lochlan moved away.

Larkin stared after him, hand on her cheek, before she turned to Matthias. Matthias had stayed where he was, watching the siblings. He waited, knowing Larkin needed to be the one to move towards him.

Larkin stared at the tall man in front of her. Who was he, Lord? I mean, really, who is he? I know his name. I know what he does for a living. But I have yet to really get to know him. Will he stick or run with the trouble we're in? Please, Lord, I need someone here on earth on my side. I've been running since I was a teen. Well, not really running, but still running. I've lost that hope I used to have in You. The hope I used to have that saw the sunny side of life, that kept me moving forward, excited to face each day. I want that back, and somehow I think this man in front of me is the one who will do it.

Larkin moved to stand in front of Matthias, eyes on his, not saying a word. When he lifted a hand, she stared at it for a moment, before searching his face again. She gave a tiny smile before placing her hand in his.

Matthias breathed a quick sigh of relief. Is she the one, Lord, the one You planned for me? She's hurting in ways I can't even imagine.

"Ready to go?" Matthias' words were quiet.

"I am. I just don't want to go back home yet. I'm scared, Matthias, more scared than I have ever been in my life."

Matthias' grip on her hand was strong as he led her towards his truck, eyes searching the area. "I know you are, my darling. I'm going to do everything I can to keep you safe." He tucked her into his truck and then slid behind the wheel. "Where you want to go?"

She shrugged, not having thought it through. "Not to Mom and Dad's. I don't want to put them at risk." She stared out the side window. "I have to go home, Matthias. My work is there."

"I know it is. But first, let's find somewhere to get something to eat. You didn't have supper and I didn't either."

She turned to him. "Food? At a time like this?"

Matthias nodded. "Yes, food. We need to eat. Where do you want to go?"

She stared at him, then shook her head. "Anywhere is okay, I guess."

"No, it's not. I'm not letting you get away with that. Where do you really want to go?"

She turned from the window. "Matthias? Oh, all right. Jonesy's is good."

"Jonesy's it is. Now, was that so hard?"

She shook her head at him. "You really do like to get your way, don't you?" There was a bitter tone to her words.

Matthias pulled the truck to the curb and threw it into park. "Larkin, let's get one thing straight. I'm not in this to get my own way. I care very much about you and want to see that you're taken care of. If you had insisted on not eating, I would have taken you home to get what you wanted and then somewhere safe. So live with it! People care about you, and you seem to just shrug it off. That's could very easily get you killed. If that doesn't matter, think about your parents and your brother. How would they feel?" His words had a bite to them Larkin hadn't heard in the short time they had known each other.

Larkin stared at him, mouth slightly open, unable to believe that he was talking to her that way. How dare he! she thought. He doesn't know me at all.

His eyes watching her, Matthias didn't move. When she didn't speak, he pulled away from the curb, heading for her house. Stopping in her driveway, he came around the truck, opened the door, and then pulled her from the truck.

"Where are your keys?" he asked, hand out for them.

She handed them to him and walked beside him to the house, her arm in his hand. He opened the door, pulled her in, then shut and locked the door. He searched to make sure no one else was there. Standing in front of her, he handed her the keys.

"I'm going home, Larkin. I really pray you realize you need help before someone dies, either you or one of your family members." He turned, walking out of the door.

She turned, shocked as the door shut behind him. How dare he, she thought. How dare he talk to me like that. Fuming she stormed into her office and threw herself into her chair, thoughts dark and troubling.

Chapter 9

Turning as he heard his name called, Matthias waited for Lochlan to catch up with him, Lochlan pointing at a local coffee shop. Seated, they exchanged idle talk until they had their order.

"Lochlan. You were looking for me?"

Lochlan nodded. "I was. Have you talked to Larkin this week?"

Matthias shook his head. "Not since I dropped her off at home that day. Why?"

"We can't reach her. We know she's been at home and at work, but she's not answering her phone and not even her door."

"Has she ever done that before?"

Lochlan sat back at the question. Then his eyes slid shut. "Yes, she has. When she was in high school, she shut down for a while. No one could get through to her, not even Edie. She was like that until she went to college. Why?"

"Because I think whatever is going on now is related to what happened then. It's not something new, not by the way she's been reacting." Matthias' eyes strayed to the window, watching the activity through it, his hand wrapped around his coffee mug. "Did she ever say what happened?"

"Never. After she had been at college, she went back more to the way she had been when she was younger but she was never the same."

"So, again I have to ask, what or who?"

Lochlan shook his head. "We could never get an answer from her. She'd give us a look and then walk away. I know Mom tried many times over the years. Edie has as well. If she was going to open up to anyone, it would be Edie."

"Tell me again about that sales rep. Did she ever say much about him?"

"The first I heard about him was the other day. I asked Mom and Dad, and they didn't have a clue either." Lochlan rubbed his thumb on his mug, a thoughtful look on his face. "I think she buried it as deep as she could."

"Someone needs to talk to her about that, to see if there is anything relevant to now. If there isn't, then we have someone new out there."

Lochlan finally looked up at Matthias, a question in his eyes. "How serious are you about Larkin, Matthias?"

Matthias shrugged. "I have no idea, Lochlan. She's shut everyone out, including me. That doesn't make for a great start to anything." He turned and looked around the cafe, his eyes stopping on a middle-aged man sitting where he could watch the two. A frown on his face, Matthias memorized as much of him as he could. "Listen. We need to find out what's going on with her. It's Saturday. What's her usual routine?"

Lochlan shrugged. "She'll do groceries and clean. She sometimes volunteers at the seniors' home in town."

Matthias' eyes shot to Lochlan. "Is today the day she would be there?"

Lochlan stared at Matthias. "It is. You don't think?"

"I do. Look, see if you can get in touch with either Bill or Andrew. Let them know this may be a link. I'll try and track her down."

Late that afternoon, Matthias sat on Larkin's front steps, waiting for her to come home. She had been one step ahead of him all day. He sighed. Was she really trying to hide from me, Lord, or is there something else going on? I really want to help her but it just doesn't seem to be working. She needs that touch from You, Lord, that touch that will renew her hope.

He heard a car pull into the driveway, a door close, and then footsteps heading his way. He didn't look up from the quarter he was moving through his fingers. He saw the sneakers stop in front of him and could feel her agitation coming at him.

"Matthias?" Larkin stood, arms full of parcels, her keys in her hand. "What are you doing here?"

"Looking for a friend I don't want to lose." He finally looked, squinting in the sun, catching a fleeting glimpse of what he wasn't sure of cross her face.

"Really?" Larkin shoved by him, her keys in the lock. Then she stopped. "I'm sorry, Matthias. You didn't deserve that."

He nodded, knowing she couldn't see him. "No, I didn't. Look, it's obvious you want to be by yourself, without any family or friends. It's good to know. Take care of yourself." He rose and headed for his vehicle.

Larkin turned, tears in her eyes, and dropped her parcels, moving to the edge of the porch. "Matthias?"

He stopped, not looking back at her, a hurt look on his face that she couldn't see and that he wouldn't show her.

"I'm so sorry. It's been a bad week and I shouldn't take it out on you. Come on in, please. We need to talk."

He turned, his eyes searching her face. "Only if you're sure."

She nodded. "I am. I shouldn't have shut you out this week."

"No, you shouldn't. Let's talk, okay, and see where we go from here. Your brother was worried enough to track me down this morning to see if I had heard from you."

She sighed. "It's so hard." She turned, gathering her parcels, and opening the door. Matthias shut it gently behind him, then stood, waiting for Larkin to return.

"Come on back to the kitchen, Matthias. I can put on some coffee for you."

He stopped in the kitchen doorway, looking around at the sunny yellow paint, off-white cabinets, and patterned countertop.

"This is nice. It's a kitchen you want to cook in."

She snorted. "If you can cook. I'm still learning."

He nodded. "My mom taught me when I was young. She told me that one day I would be on my own and I needed to know. And she said besides that it would impress my date or my wife if I could whip up a special meal without burning anything."

Larkin spun, not quite sure if he was serious. "She actually said that? Your mom sounds like a special lady."

"She was, Larkin. That she was."

She handed him his coffee mug, then pointed back to the living room. "Let's sit in there." She grabbed a bottle of juice for herself.

He sat, watching as she moved restlessly around the room, not quite sure how he should proceed.

"Larkin?" When she turned, he asked, "You said it was a bad week?"

She nodded. "It has been." She sighed, then sat on the couch beside him, her back to the arm and a pillow wrapped in her arms. "I talked to the other OT's. They've found out that Eve hasn't been honest with us, has been sending business away from us. We are also having a forensic audit done on the books as John thinks she may have been skimming from us. It's so sad, Matthias. We never expected this from her."

"I would think not. Did you find out where that referral came from?"

She nodded. "Eve. Somehow she dummied up the referral and used the old address. I've talked to Alice. She has no need of occupational therapy or speech pathology and was shocked that a referral had been made for her."

"If she did one, how many others has she done?" Matthias stared at the floor, sick at the ramifications of that.

"I know. We're going back over all our referrals, particularly the ones where we couldn't get any response to our calls." She stared at the ceiling for a moment, then looked at Matthias. "I just haven't had time to call you or Bill or Andrew. Our group has been meeting every night going over everything. It involves you now. We have no idea how far it reaches."

Matthias nodded. "It will likely reach into any area that takes you into a private home. Have you talked to Julia?"

"Julia? Oh, the physiotherapist. No, I haven't. I don't know her well enough."

Matthias grinned as he pulled out his phone. "Mark? Hey, how's it going? Is that right?   That's great.   Listen, I have a question for Julia. What's that? She's not home? That's okay. Just ask her if in the past six months or so, she's been asked to see someone in a private home and no one has responded to her calls or visits. I know.

It's complicated. With me? We're working on that. Larkin and her other OT's too. Sure, she can call me or she can call Larkin. Here's her number. What no pen? That's unusual for you." Matthias laughed, then pocketed his phone.

Larkin stared at him. "You know Julia?"

"I do. She's married to a good friend of mine, Mark. They go to your church."

"Is there anyone here you don't know?"

Matthias started laughing again, then sobered. "Plenty of people. It's just we have a group of eight really good friends from college. Mark, Josiah, Zeke all married ladies from here. Bill's friends with all of us as well. Jason, too, now because of Julia. Andrew's just sort of drifted in as well."

"Wow! I don't think I've ever had that many close friends. Most of the ones I had are married or moved away. That changes it, you know."

"I know it does, but Faith, Julia, and Paige would really like to be your friend. Give them a chance."

She slowly nodded. "I'll try but it's hard, Matthias. No one knows how hard."

Matthias reached for her, drawing her into his arms. She resisted and he kept his arms loose until she finally relaxed against him.

"What happened, Larkin? What happened to you that destroyed your hope and your trust?"

She laid her head on his shoulder and he felt the tears soak into his shirt. "I've never talked about it, Matthias. Not to Mom, Dad. Not Lochlan. Edie has guessed some of it but not the whole thing."

"Then, tell me. Whatever it is, I promise, I won't let you go, won't hurt you. If not today, then one day soon. Your timing. If it relates to what we're going through, then sooner is better." He reached for a tissue and handed it to her.

Larkin felt safe in Matthias' arm, probably for the first time in years. She turned her head to look up at him.

"I can trust you, Matthias. It just hurts so much."

"What does?"

"When I worked for Edie, there was another rep who used to come in. He was older, in his 30's I think. He always tried to get me to go out with him. When I refused, he grew nasty, to the point if I saw him coming, I would hide in the back and let Edie deal with him. I should have told her. She would have sent him packing before anything happened."

Matthias waited, not quite sure what she was going to say, but sick at heart that anyone wanted to hurt her.

"One day he came in when Edie was out and I had no choice but to speak with him. I tried to tell him that Edie would be back and he needed to talk with her. He refused. He grabbed me by the arms and squeezed. Told me I was going out with him and back to his house afterwards. If I didn't he would hurt my parents and my brother. Somehow I broke free and ran from him. Edie came in just after I ran out and sent him on his way. She asked but I couldn't say anything. He had threatened that if I said anything he'd hurt everyone I knew. I never saw him again, so I don't know what happened. I've been living in fear that I'll run into him. He's from the area."

Matthias' arms tightened around Larkin and his head came down on hers.

"He should have been charged, Larkin. I know you were scared and that makes me sick that someone would threaten you in such a way. Do you have his name?"

She nodded. "I never forgot it. I'll give it to Bill or Andrew and they can look into him."

"How old were you?"

He felt her draw deeper into his arms. "I was only 16, Matthias. Too young for that."

"We'll find him, Larkin. We'll make him understand what he did was wrong. This is what changed you, isn't it?"

She nodded. "I was so scared, Matthias, I couldn't think. I couldn't tell anyone. I realize now that was part of what he was trying to do but at the time I didn't."

"We'll do our best to keep you safe." He tilted his head to look down at her. "How about dinner?"

"Dinner?"

"Yeah, you know. That meal you eat in the afternoon." He grinned as she shook her head at him.

"I have some meat in the fridge we can barbecue and there's some veggies to go on as well." She went to stand. He hadn't let go of her. "Matthias?"

"Yes, my darling?"

"I need to stand up."

He laughed. "I know you do. I just want you to remember you're safe with me. If anything comes up, not matter how trivial, talk to me."

She stared at him and then nodded. "Thank you."

Chapter 10

Larkin looked around at the other members of her group. She could feel the anger in the group. Sighing, she looked down at her paperwork. It wasn't good. Eve had done a number on their books and their referrals.

"So, where do we stand, Tom?" She looked down at the man sitting at the end of the table.

"Not where we should be, that's for sure. I've taken everything we've discovered and passed it on to the police. They're bringing in a forensic accountant to go over everything. Right now, it's thousands of dollars billed to private insurance companies that we will have to repay somehow."

There were murmurs around the table. Then Larkin spoke.

"We've given this to the police. We'll let the insurance companies know that it was an ex-employee who committed the fraud and that it is now a police investigation. We are agreed on that?" Nods came from all at the table. "Then, John, you and I will be speaking with the attorney we talked to. We need to work with the police in this investigation and then with the insurance companies. Don't panic yet. Wait to see what the accountant uncovers first. Our next meeting is next Monday, correct?" Again, nods came from everyone. "Okay, then let's go do what we do best, taking care of our patients."

John stopped Larkin from walking away. "Larkin, I know you moved your office home while you were going through some stuff. If you want to move back, we'd love to have you here."

Larkin stared up at John for a moment, then shook her head. "Not yet, John. There's still something going on that we haven't quite figured out, that has nothing to do with Eve that we can see as yet. Until I know for sure being here won't risk your lives, I'd rather not."

John nodded. "That's okay, then. We just wanted you to know we missed having you around here and want you back when you can come back." He squeezed her shoulder, then turned and walked away.

Larkin stared after him, remembering to keep her mouth closed. What was that all about, Lord? They've never spoken like that to me before. She shook her head in disbelief, then headed for her car.

Her footsteps slowed as she approached it, then made her way around it. She shook her head, anger spreading through her. Four flat tires! And sliced into, she could tell. She pulled out her phone to make the call, turning in a circle as she felt watched. Where was he or she, she thought? Why do we always expect it to be a man? Lord, protect me, please.

Jason made his way to Larkin, wending his way through the crime scene team and the waiting tow truck.

"Larkin?"

Larkin spun, surprise evident on her face. "Jason? What are you doing here?"

He pulled her off to one side, away from the activity. "I'm here because we have an active investigation about you underway. When I heard your call, I headed over here. Talk to me."

She shrugged, eyes on her car. "What's to say? I was in a meeting, came out and found that." Her index finger stabbed at the car. "Now who would do that?"

"That's what I would like to know. Listen, have you come up with any more names for us?"

She stared at him. "Any more names?" her voice rising as she finished. "Jason, I have no idea who would do this. I have given you any names I know. This is really beyond what I would have expected. I shouldn't have even been here today, except that we called a meeting about Eve and the investigation. I don't work from this office any more, so why would someone track me here?" She was almost in tears as she finished.

Jason studied her, then the people standing around. "Take a look at the people here, Larkin. Tell me who you recognize. Then we'll work from there."

"Recognize? Jason!" She shook her head, then turned. "All the OTs have left, so there isn't anyone here I know. Does that help?" She was getting sarcastic.

"Larkin! Enough already! We're doing our best to solve the investigation and find out who is responsible. An attitude like that doesn't help." He had to bite back more words, words that wouldn't get him the answers he wanted.

"I'm done here, Jason. I can't help you any more. It looks as if my car won't be ready for a while." She sighed. "Now, I have to find a way home."

"I'll take you. I'm having your car towed to our garage and the techs will go over it there. Hopefully by this time tomorrow you'll have it back." Hand to her back, he directed her to his car and closed the door behind her.

"Jason?"

He turned as a tech approached for a quiet word, then slid into the front seat.

"Jason?" Larkin's voice was quiet.

"Yeah, Larkin?"

"What was that about?"

He stared out the window, fingers tapping the steering wheel, before he started the car and pulled away, heading for her home.

"It's a good thing you didn't try and get into your car. There was a bomb inside, rigged to go off if you opened the front door. Our tech caught it before anyone was hurt."

Her face white, Larkin's hand went to her mouth. "Jason? Why? Who?"

"That's what we need to figure out, Larkin. That's why we keep asking you if you have any enemies or can give us any names."

She shook in fear. "I don't know any more names, Jason." She stared out the side window, then reached to swipe at the tears on her face. He handed her a tissue and she crumpled it in her hand.

"Are you safe at your home, Larkin, or do I need to take you somewhere else?"

She shook her head. "It doesn't matter, Jason. It doesn't look as if I'm safe anywhere, does it?"

Jason didn't speak, pulling into her driveway, then turning to her. "Let me walk through your house and yard first, okay? Your keys. Do you have an alarm system?" At her nod, he continued, "I'll need your password, then. I'm locking the doors behind me. Stay here, no matter what happens."

She waited, eyes on her home, suddenly feeling very unsafe. Her phone chimed, causing her to jump, hand going to her chest as her heart raced. She scanned the phone. Matthias!

"Hello?"

"Larkin? Are you okay?"

"Matthias, no, I'm not. My car had four flats and then Jason said the tech found a bomb in it. He's here going through my house right now!"

"Where are you?" He sounded as if he was running.

"In his cruiser. Are you running?"

"I am. I'm heading your way."

"That isn't necessary, Matthias. I'm fine. Jason's here."

"It doesn't matter. I'm five minutes away now."

Jason unlocked the doors and opened Larkin's. "I need you to come with me and go through your house. I can't tell if anything has been moved."

Larkin stood, staring at him. "Jason? You're scaring me."

"I don't mean to, but we can't be too careful, Larkin, not given what just happened." He looked up as he heard a vehicle stop. "Matthias is here?"

She nodded as she turned to watch the road. "He just called and said he was coming. Is that a problem?"

Jason shook his head. "It shouldn't be. I just didn't expect him here so soon."

"Did you call him? If you didn't, then who did?"

"I don't think anyone did, Larkin. I think he is so concerned that he was on his way here just to make sure you were okay."

Matthias stopped at the end of the cruiser, eyes shifting between the two in front of him, before he moved to stand beside Larkin.

"Jason? What's going on?"

"Nothing, I hope, but I do want Larkin to come through her house. Something feels off, but I'm not familiar with her home."

Larkin reached for Matthias' hand, her fingers cold as she gripped tight. "Matthias, please walk with me."

"Not a problem, my darling. Come. Let's walk through and see what Jason felt."

Larkin stopped as she entered, her eyes searching, a frown on her face. "There's something missing here, Jason. But what?"

Matthias studied the hallway. "There was a photo on the wall, Larkin."

She blanched. "That's a family photo, Jason. Why would someone want that?"

Jason pulled out his notepad, jotting that down. "Every time you see something missing or even think it is, tell me."

By the time she had gone through her home, there were a dozen items on Jason's list.

"Who would have done this, Jason? The house was alarmed, doors locked."

Jason stepped away to look at her alarm, then opened the door and walked to the window, before coming back inside.

"No one could see you punching in your code. You had a strong code, I take it?" At her nod, he continued, "Would it be something someone could easily figure out if they knew you or your habits?"

She shook her head. "Not at all. Not even Lochlan would have been able to figure it out."

"Okay. So that means it was hacked in some way. Now we just have to figure out how." He stared at the control panel, then pried off the cover, staring at the insides of it. He pulled out his pen, working away at something inside. "This is how. Someone put this inside and it tracked your password very easily." He dropped it into an evidence bag. "I'll take this to the lab, but I doubt we'll find much on it." He tapped the cover back into place. "Now reset your password to something totally different."

Larkin looked between the two men, seeing the grim looks on their faces. "Now what? Am I safe here?"

"I think you are, Larkin, for tonight anyway." Jason walked back through the house, checking the windows. "I'll have a patrol car pass by more often that we usually do. Don't hesitate to call 911 if you are at all afraid. Matthias, can I talk to you outside for a moment?"

Larkin watched the two men converse, before Jason headed for his cruiser. Matthias walked slowly back into the house, face thoughtful.

"Matthias?"

His head raised at her voice. "Larkin, what am I going to do with you? I leave you alone and you get yourself into more trouble?"

"Get myself into more trouble? Matthias!" Then she caught the sparkle of mischief in his eyes and shook her head. "Will I ever be able to tell when you're teasing me?"

"I certainly hope you do. Now, what can I do to help you feel safer?"

She turned, wrapping her arms around herself and paced through her home. "I still feel like something's off in here, Matthias. Did Jason look for any cameras or hidden microphones or anything like that?"

Matthias stopped following her at her question. "I don't think so, Larkin. Is there a reason you're asking?"

She shrugged. "In all the movies, that's what they always find. I wouldn't have a clue what to look for."

Matthias studied her for a moment. "Pack a bag and gather what you need for the next few days. I'm taking you somewhere safe."

She spun, shaking her head, then stopped at the look on his face. "You really mean that, don't you?"

"I do. Go on. Get what you need."

She nodded and moved to do what he asked.

Chapter 11

Matthias tucked Larkin into his truck later that week, eyes searching the area around him, before he slid behind the wheel. He pulled away from the house they had just seen a patient in and headed for his home.

"Larkin, where are you planning on spending the weekend?"

She shrugged. "Jason's gone through my house and says it should be okay to return home. He's having my car delivered tonight."

"Okay, then. That's good. What about stopping for something to eat? I know it's early yet, but if we eat, then I can take you straight to your house."

She stared through the side window, thoughts confused. "Why are you doing this, Matthias?"

"Doing what?" His eyes watched the vehicle following him, taking every turn he did.

"Being so nice to me when I've brought danger to you."

He shook his head, shooting her a quick glance. "A couple of things to consider. One, you didn't bring danger to me. I was lured out to that place the same way you were. Two, you're a friend I've come to treasure. Three, there's something between us I'd like to explore, if you're willing. Just think about it. I'll not push."

She studied his face, then nodded. "Thank you, Matthias, for being who you are." She watched as he kept flicking a look at the rearview mirror and finally turned to stare behind them. "Are we being followed?"

"It seems as if we are. Whoever it is stays far enough back that I can't get a plate number."

Larkin pulled out a camera, causing Matthias to stare at her for a few seconds.

"I always carry a camera, just in case I see something I like. I can get really good close-ups with it." She fiddled with the settings as she watched the vehicle hang back, then sat forward again, scanning through her photos. "I got it, Matthias," she stated, a little smugness coming through.

"Good." He laughed at the look on her face. "Now send it to Bill. You do have his phone number, don't you?"

"I do. Now, what do we do?"

"We go for a meal somewhere and wait for Bill to get back to us." He pulled into a local restaurant, then came around to help her down, not letting go of her hand as they walked towards the restaurant."

Seated at a table, Matthias looked around, his glance going to the door whenever it opened.

Larkin pulled out her phone as it chimed. "It's Bill. He's checked the plate." She sighed as she read his message. "About what you'd figure. The vehicle is reported stolen." She picked up her phone again as another message came in. "Oh, good. He had officers searching for it and they've found it. Is it over, do you think?" She looked at Matthias with hope in her eyes.

Matthias sighed as their orders were placed in front of them. He didn't want to destroy the hope she had but he knew better.

"I don't think so, Larkin. Dig into your meal before it gets cold. The food is good here." He took a bite of his steak and chewed, a thoughtful look on his face. "These are likely low-level guys, probably don't even know who the boss is."

She stared down at her roast chicken dinner, her fork moving slowly through the mashed potatoes. "That's about what I thought you'd say. I want this over, Matthias, and over yesterday."

"You and me both, Larkin. You and me both." He paused, his hesitation not like him. "Larkin, tomorrow is Saturday. Would you spend the day with me? Let me take you somewhere we can spend a day having fun without worrying about what's hanging over us?"

"Why?"

"Why? Because I want to spend time with you, to get to know you better. Is that a problem?"

She stared at him, reading the sincerity in his eyes and something else that set her heart pounding. Lord, what's going on here? I'm in the middle of something I have no idea where's it going and You bring

Matthias into my life. I know You have a plan and purpose for me, one I just haven't found yet. Don't let me go wrong this time.

She finally nodded. "Okay. Where?"

He grinned at her, seeing the apprehension lurking in her eyes. "Wear causal clothes and walking shoes. I have a spot I like to go to that settles my heart back down and brings perspective back to my life."

Larkin's phone chimed again and she ignored it, her focus on Matthias. "Thank you, Matthias. You're so sweet."

He choked on his water. "Now that's something I haven't been called in a long time."

The next morning, Larkin stared at the buildings in front of her, her thoughts wondering as to why Matthias brought her to a pioneer village.

"Why here, Matthias?" She tried to pull her hand from his but his grip tightened as he grinned down at her.

"Because in the busyness of our lives today, I need to be reminded of simpler times. Times when faith, family and friends were what mattered most, not money or rushing to the next thrill. Have you ever been here before?"

She shook her head. "No, I haven't. In fact, I not likely would have come if you hadn't brought me. History wasn't my thing."

"This isn't about history, Larkin, as much as it is about learning how people survived, lived, and loved. Come on. You'll surprise yourself at how much you'll enjoy it. Then I have somewhere else to take you."

Larkin turned to him, searching his face, once more seeing something in his eyes. Lord, I can't do this, she thought. I can't let anyone close to me, but he's getting through all my defenses and walls.

Later that morning, Larkin stood in the church on the site, staring at the simple pews, then walking forward to the pulpit. Her hand ran along the rough wood. Matthias watched, seeing the change that had come over during the few hours they had spent there. Thank you, Lord, she needed this, a time where she didn't have to be afraid of anyone, didn't have to run from someone.

Larkin looked up at Matthias standing in front of her and smiled. "You were right, Matthias. I did need this. Now where?"

He reached for her hand and she willing placed hers in his. She had come to trust him that morning in a way that she didn't trust anyone else. Was hope springing back up in my heart, Lord, she asked?

Matthias tucked her into his truck, his eyes watchful. He hadn't seen anyone that he would suspect and he hadn't heard anything from Jason or Bill over the morning. He had had a long talk with them both the night before about plans to catch the ones after them and both the officers were working on them.

"Now, I get to take you to another favourite spot, but let's eat first."

"Eat? I don't see any restaurants around here."

He grinned at her as he pulled away, heading for the river. "I packed a picnic lunch. Remember, I said I could cook."

She snorted. "You just want to impress me, right?"

He shook his head even as he laughed. "Not a chance, Larkin. That's not my plan, but if it works, what can I say?"

Her laughter rang through the cab of the truck, free from any lingering doubt or pain for once. "You're crazy, you know that?"

"I know." He parked, then came around to help her down, reaching into the back of the back and pulling out a picnic basket and blanket. "Come on. I want to show you another favourite spot."

Larkin sat back on the blanket, her eyes watching the river in front of her, her body relaxing. Matthias watched her, his heart in his eyes without realizing it. He sighed to himself. How was he to keep this special lady safe?

Larkin finally turned, her eyes searching Matthias' face. "Thank you, Matthias. This has been just wonderful."

"You're welcome. You have relaxed. I don't know if I've seen you this relaxed."

She snorted, drawing a laugh from him. "Not likely. We've had too much going on. Now what?"

"You mean you just don't want to sit here and watch the river?"

She shook her head, a slight smile on her face. "You promised to show me somewhere else."

He nodded, then gathered up the remains of their lunch, helping her to stand. She folded up the blanket before he reached for her hand. Tucking her inside his truck, he stood for a moment, looking around. Something was off, he thought.

His phone chiming startled him and he reached for it.

"Hey, Bill. You're still working?" He listened, his eyes searching the area around him. He sighed as he pocketed his phone. So much for the rest of their day.

Larkin studied him as he slid into the truck. "Matthias?"

He finally turned to her. "Larkin, Bill just called. It's wasn't good news. Your alarm went off and they couldn't get in touch with you. There's been a fire at your home."

She paled. "A fire?" She reached for her phone. "Oh, no! I muted it last night to sleep and forgot it this morning." She searched his face. "How bad?"

"Bill didn't say. I'm taking you home to see."

Larkin stood behind the police lines, her eyes on her home, Matthias' arm around her. Bill approached, not quite sure how to talk to her.

"Bill? How bad is it?"

"Smoke and water damage in the kitchen area, Larkin. The fire was set at the back door. Somehow they managed to get through the new lock you set up on the gate, and I would like to know how."

"Is my office okay?"

He nodded. "I'll have the fire captain escort you in soon so you can get your work and laptop, but you won't be staying here until it's repaired. Where will you go?"

She shrugged. "I have no idea. I don't want to take this to my parents or Lochlan."

Bill and Matthias exchanged a glance, before Matthias spoke.

"I have a little guest cottage on my property, Larkin. You're welcome to use it for now."

She turned, eyes once more searching his face, before she nodded. "Might as well, I guess, seeing as whoever it is tends to want to go after both of us."

"No, Larkin, he's never been after me. It's been you all along." Matthias watched as the realization hit her.

She stared at him, tears gathering in her eyes. "Then, I can't. I can't bring this to you."

"Yes, you can. Together, we'll figure it out."

Chapter 12

Walking out of the library four days later, Larkin hesitated as to which way to go. She needed to go to her house to meet the insurance adjustor, but that wasn't for a while. She couldn't meet with Matthias - he was with a client. She sighed. He had become a big portion of her life, she thought.

She turned to walk away from the area and stopped, two men in hoodies and sunglasses standing in front of her. She felt someone behind her and fear rose.

"It's okay, Larkin. We're not going to hurt you. We just want to talk with you for a moment." The man reached for her arm and pulled her around behind the library.

Larkin tried to pull away, but couldn't. Fear rose in her and she shook from the intensity of it.

The man stopped, staring behind her before nodding.

"Larkin, you part of a group of paramedical professionals who have been targeted by someone in town. We don't have enough evidence to go to the police, but this person has decided that anyone who is in a profession other than a physician has to pay. We're working on that."

"Just who are you?" She stared between the two men standing in front of her, a frown on her face. His voice sounded familiar, but she couldn't quite place it.

"We're friends, Larkin. We want to help you stop what's going on directed at your friends and colleagues."

"You mean Matthias and I?"

The second man shook his head and spoke. "You and Matthias are taking the brunt of it for some reason that we can't figure out. But others have been targeted as well. We know Eve has been part of the group but we don't know how far up the chain she is." He handed her a large envelope. "This is what we've discovered so far. Use it to bring this to a conclusion, if you can."

The two men stared behind her again, and she heard footsteps walking away from there. As the two men walked in the opposite direction, she turned. Of course, the person behind her was gone. That was par for the course, she thought. She studied the envelope in her hand and sighed. It would have to wait. She had to meet that adjustor now.

The man who had been behind Larkin pulled his hoodie down and settled his ball cap back on his head. He didn't want to be recognized in a town he was well-known in. He headed for his car, stopping before he pulled the door open. Lord, I have no idea how many more will face what four men have faced already. Please keep them safe. Bring this to a resolution. He slid behind his wheel and left.

Matthias stood at the front door of Larkin's house, his eyes scanning the area around her home. He, like Bill, wanted to know how the man or woman had gotten through the lock on her gate. It was a numbered lock, so it wasn't picked. He headed for the back yard, his hands running along the fence. He stopped at the back corner. Just what he thought. The boards were loose.

"Bill? Matthias. Yeah, I'm at Larkin's. She's with the adjustor now. Listen, I found out how they keep getting into her backyard. There are loose boards on the back fence, the nails barely into the wood. No, I'm serious. You know she backs onto a farmer's field."

Matthias could hear Bill in the background, then his voice came back strong.

"Matthias, I'm sending out a crime scene tech. Can you wait and show him the area?"

"I can. Look, Larkin's finished, so she'll be wanting to pack up some stuff likely. Call me if there's a change in timing."

"Will do and thanks for finding that."

Larkin approached Matthias, a question in her eyes.

"Matthias?"

"Larkin." Matthias reached to pull her into a hug. "Get everything settled?"

She nodded, then rested her head on his chest. "I did. It's going to take a few weeks more, he said. I'll have to order new cabinets, flooring, appliances. They'll have to paint throughout as well from the smoke." She sighed. "There's stuff that I need to go through and that means our Saturday won't happen."

"Sure, it will. I'll be here working right alongside you. Josiah and Faith, Mark and Julia, and Zeke and Paige have all offered to help as have Jonah, Samuel and Adam. Noah wishes he could but he's stuck overseas again."

"Why?"

"Why what?"

"Why do they want to help?"

"Because you're my friend and that's what they do."

She finally nodded. "What were you doing back here?"

"Waiting for a crime scene tech. I found out how whoever it is got into your yard. And there's Nelson now."

"What do you have, Matthias? Bill seemed to think you solved the mystery for us." Nelson shook hands with the two.

"I did. The boards are loose in that corner. It's almost as if they were loosened and then set back in place."

Nelson took a look and then pulled one away from the bracing. "You're right, Matthias. Unfortunately, it's been too long to get any footprints but maybe they left some evidence. If you two want to wait near the house or in the house, I'll be about thirty minutes or less."

Matthias seated Larkin at a table in the local cafe before sliding into a chair across from her. Nelson hadn't found a lot but had taken some samples.

"Tell me again about the three men." Matthias watched as she played with her silverware.

"There was something about them, Matthias. I know them, but I couldn't put a name to them. I couldn't get a good look at them what with the hoodies and the sunglasses. And I didn't see the man behind him. At least I am assuming it was a man."

"They're from town. Now, I wonder." Matthias' voice dropped away.

"Wonder what."

"Josiah, Mark and Zeke each mentioned being approached by a group of men asking for help in cleaning up the town. They weren't vigilantes, but wanted to work within the law."

Larkin shrugged as she eyed her salad. "Tell me again why I ordered a salad."

Matthias started to laugh. "I have no idea, but tell you what. You share your salad with me and I'll share my burger and fries."

"Now that I can agree with." She dipped a fry into ketchup and then chewed on it. "What time are your friends coming around on Saturday?"

"Around 10." He watched her face. "No need to be nervous, Larkin."

She sighed. "It's so hard, Matthias. I have trouble making friends. I never used to, but I just don't seem to be able to make friends as an adult, and I don't know why."

Matthias reached for her hand and held it. "There's nothing wrong with you, Larkin. Look, you made friends with me, didn't you?" A spark of mischief appeared in his eyes.

She shot a glance up at him and then laughed. "Yeah, I did, didn't I? And you're not so scary after all."

"Thanks, I think."

Larkin finally straightened up and rubbed her back. It was late afternoon on Saturday and with the help of Matthias' friends, who now claimed her as their friend, they had accomplished what she needed to do. Carpets were pulled up, furniture had been vacuumed and cleaned. Bags of clothing were ready to head to the washer. Jonah and Adam had removed her appliances and gotten rid of them, where she had no idea.

"Thanks, everyone. I couldn't have done it without your help."

Josiah stood with his arm draped around Faith. "Not a problem, Larkin. Now, Uncle Seth has been brewing and cooking all day for us. Let's head back to our place for a meal."

Larkin went to protest, then stopped when she saw the look on Faith's face. She moved forward to hug Faith.

"We'll be glad to, but we're awful dirty."

Faith laughed. "That's okay. We have plenty of showers between the two houses and lots of time."

Andrew looked at Bill, then back at the papers he had been handed, not quite believing what Bill had said.

"You've investigated this thoroughly, I know, Bill, but who would have thought."

"I know. The last person I would have figured to be involved. Now I just have to find the evidence, and that seems to be very well hidden."

"It will be. For now, you're the one working on it, no one else. If we need someone else, pull in Jason."

Bill nodded as he watched Andrew walk away. He's tired, Lord, carrying too much of a load right now. Give him the strength he needs and please Lord, bring a lady into his life. Bill didn't know Andrew's background all that well. Andrew just never spoke about it. He sighed and turned back to his office, facing what he felt was an insurmountable task.

Chapter 13

*S*taring at the apples in the bin in front of her, Larkin stood lost in thought, finally sighing and reaching to fill the bag she had in her hand. Something was off today and she just couldn't put her finger on it. Maybe it was because she was out of her own home. Maybe it was because she was living too close to Matthias at the moment and needed a break to assess what her feelings for him was. Maybe it was just everything.

She headed for her parents' for a while and then back to her own home, walking through it. It had been two weeks since the fire and it still looked the same as when Matthias and his friends had helped clear it out. The painters were to start next week. She had to go furniture shopping but had no desire to do that.

Finally, sitting down on the small couch, she laid her head back and stared at the ceiling. She felt a sense of impending doom and she didn't like it one bit. She reached for her Bible and searching found the passages on hope the pastor had given her. I'm too far gone, Lord. I don't think I'll ever have that hope again. She sat, silence surrounding her, focusing on that word. What is hope, she questioned? Lord, I need answers and I just don't seem to be able to find them. Why? It seems everything is going wrong and I have nowhere to turn but to You. Is that what this is all about, Lord? Bringing me back to you? There must have been an easier way.

She finally reached for a pad of paper and a pen and starting jotting down thoughts and ideas, her mind racing ahead of her pen. Who was behind this? Who stood to gain? And why? She finally set the pad and pen aside and reached for the blanket on the back of the couch. Fatigue had set in and she needed that nap.

Matthias stood on his back deck, mug of coffee in hand, and watched the cottage. He knew Larkin was really struggling at this point and he had no idea of how to help her. His phone chimed and he pulled it out. Bill needed to speak with him without Larkin. Now what, he wondered?

He turned as he heard footsteps and Bill appeared, holding up a paperbag from their favourite cafe.

"I brought food." Bill's grin lit up his face.

"Sounds good. Sit." Matthias pointed at the table. "What did you want, Bill?"

"Let's eat, then talk." Bill stared down at his sandwich. "On second thought, maybe this isn't such a good idea."

"What? Eating first?"

Bill shook his head. "I don't know. Matthias, we've found out who one of the top men are, and I know Larkin's going to be hurt very badly."

Matthias wiped his mouth, then stared across at the cottage. "Do we need to go talk to her?"

Bill shook his head. "We will. But first I need to find out some more information."

"Not happening, Bill. Larkin will never forgive us if we don't tell her what we know now. I can't take that risk with her."

Bill looked up at Matthias, his eyes thoughtful. "It's like that, is it, Matthias?"

Matthias sighed. "Not yet, Bill, but heading that way on my part. She's a good friend, and I won't have her hurt because we're holding things back."

Bill nodded. "Let's eat, then you go get her. She's home, is she?"

"She is. She was out for quite a while this morning. She's exhausted. I can see it in the way she's moving. This is taking a big toll on her."

Matthias tapped at Larkin's door a few minutes later, waiting for her to answer. He tapped again and then heard her muttering as she came towards the door.

Popping it open, Larkin glared at Matthias. "You just had to knock, didn't you?"

Matthias stared at her. "I'm sorry, Larkin. I had no idea you were sleeping. Bill's here and wants to talk to us both."

She continued to glare at him. "Really? Doesn't he take any time off at all?" She sighed. "Give me a couple of minutes." She slammed the door in his face.

Matthias shook his head even as he grinned to himself. She was ticked, he could tell.

Larkin opened the door carefully and stepped out. "I'm sorry. I shouldn't have taken it out on you."

"That's fine, Larkin. Come here." Matthias wrapped her in a hug, just holding her for a few minutes until he felt her relax. He stepped back, watching her face, then reached for her hand. "Come on. Let's find out what Bill has to say. Who knows? Maybe he's solved the mystery and we can go on with our lives."

She snorted. "Not highly likely, Matthias. I can feel someone out there, watching us, just waiting, ready to strike when we least expect it." She tightened her hand on Matthias as they walked across the grass.

Bill stood, watching them, a speculative look on his face he quickly hid. Another one, Lord? Another friend with a lady he found when they were both in trouble? Bless them, Lord. Help us to solve this.

Larkin sat, her eyes not moving from Bill, who stared back at her.

"Bill? Matthias said you had news. Solved it yet?"

Bill choked on his coffee, then spoke. "Not quite yet, Larkin. We're still working angles and people. But we have located one person who is involved."

"Who?"

Bill stared past her, gathering his thoughts. "Bob Edwards?"

"Bobby?" She was surprised. "I don't believe that." She shook her head. "There's no way he would be."

"I'm sorry, Larkin, but we have irrefutable proof that he is."

Her head went down on her folded arms. "Why? He's rich."

"Not he's not, Larkin." Bill watched as she raised her head to stare at him. "Not any more. He's been divorced twice, has three kids. The spousal and child support eat into his wages. Besides, our evidence shows he has a drug problem."

"Bobby?" At his nod, she stood and walked away.

Matthias watched her. "How good is the evidence, Bill?"

"Good enough that we could arrest him tonight and put him away for years. He's dealing as well, not just using."

Matthias nodded towards Larkin. "Give her a few moments. It's going take time for her to absorb that."

"It will. Now, I understand she had an encounter with some townsfolk the other day."

Matthias turned to Bill. "Did she tell you that?"

"No, she didn't. One of our undercover officers was near and heard the conversation."

"And?"

Bill shook his head. "If I tell you, please let her tell you herself. You didn't hear anything from me." He stared down at his mug. "They're not vigilantes, I would gather. Just men who want to clean up their town. She's not the first one they've talked to."

Matthias' eyes shot to Bill. "They're not? Let me guess, Josiah, Mark, Zeke, or their ladies?"

"I would suspect that's the case. I can't say for sure. None of them have said."

Larkin dropped back into her chair, her eyes on Bill. "What proof do you have?"

"Enough that we could arrest him tonight, Larkin. He's a dealer too."

She shook her head. "So how does he fit into what's going on?"

"Blackmail, more than likely. At least, that's what we've been told."

She shook her head. "I would never have thought of him. How does that affect us?"

"We're still working on connecting all the pieces, but he knows Eve."

She sighed, then shook her head once again. "It all comes back to Eve, doesn't it? Have you figured out why?"

"Not yet. That lady doesn't seem to have a background."

"What do you mean?" Matthias spoke up.

"Just what I said. No background. She doesn't exist before she took the job here."

Larkin sat back abruptly, her hand on her cheek. "Doesn't exist? How is that possible?"

Bill shrugged. "That we're working on, Larkin." He held up a hand. "I know I'm saying that a lot, but that's what an investigation is. Lots of legwork and looking into things."

He stood, staring at the two before his eyes raised to study the sky. "I don't need to tell you two to be very careful. This is always a dangerous part of any investigation. We're getting there but we don't have all the pieces yet. We don't have the key piece or leader that we need."

Chapter 14

The man stood in the back of the church, watching Matthias and Larkin as they stood after the service talking with friends. He glanced around, then back at the two. He exited the building, searching for one of their vehicles. Seeing Matthias', he headed that way. Stooping for a moment, he straightened and walked away to his vehicle parked hear the front of the lot.

Matthias tucked Larkin into his truck, then stopped, eyes searching, feeling himself being watched. He slid behind the wheel, and turned to her.

"Lunch out or are you going to your parents?"

"Either is fine. Mom doesn't care."

"Then how be we head to your parents for now and then split later and go for a walk along the river?"

"I like that idea, Matthias. Lochlan and Angeline will be there."

"Angeline?"

She laughed. "You haven't heard? Lochlan has a girlfriend."

"That's why he hasn't been around much lately."

"That would do it."

Later, Matthias reached for Larkin's hand as they walked the bank of the river, his eyes on her face, seeing the effects stress was having on her.

"Are you doing okay?"

Larkin turned at his words, her eyes on his. "I would say yes, but I won't lie to you, Matthias. You don't deserve that. I'm struggling to see God's hand in this. I get up my hope that it will be over soon, and something else happens."

"I know. I can see you struggling. I've been praying for you. Talk to me when you get really low, okay?"

She nodded. "I will. Now, let's leave that behind us for the afternoon, can we?"

"That we can." He pointed to the other bank. "Have you ever walked that side?"

She shook her head. "Not for years. I haven't been here much lately. Life got too busy and too much in the way."

She stopped, staring at the water. "Matthias, why did you move to this area?"

He stared at her for a moment. "I went to college in Oak City, as you know. I really like this area. Noah's from here and convinced the other seven of us to stay here. I'm glad I did. If I had gone elsewhere, I wouldn't have met you."

She glanced up at him, expecting to see what she wasn't sure. Searching his face and eyes, she nodded. "It's home, isn't it? Not a lot of places feel like that, do they?"

"No, they don't. I could have gone back home. In fact I was offered a job there half way through my course, but I turned it down. It wasn't where God wanted me."

"How did you know for sure about that?"

"How did I know what? Where God wanted me? I prayed lots, talked to friends and mentors, my foster parents. He kept closing doors to opportunities, or I didn't have the peace I needed to resettle somewhere. Here I had peace. I know without a shadow of a doubt He planned this for me."

"I wish I had that confidence. I came here because it's where I grew up and I was too scared to go elsewhere. I commuted to Oak City every day. I'm not brave enough to venture far from home."

"You are. You just haven't drawn down deep enough. I'm not saying you haven't trusted God enough. Only you can decide that. But something crushed you in the past. You lost hope in life, lost belief in yourself, and your trust in others." He felt her eyes on him as he continued. "I can see, little by little, you're gaining strength and trust. You're coming into who you can be, Larkin." His eyes locked on hers. "I like what I see and would like to get to know that lady."

She sighed. "You won't like her at all. She's brutally honest."

Matthias laughed as he swept her into his arms. "Honest I can take. Don't ever hide from me, Larkin. My heart can take what you dish out."

"I know you can. I just feel like I'm dumping so much on you right now."

"Don't ever feel that way. We're in this together, Larkin-love. Somehow, God brought us together. We'll make it to the end."

She nodded against him, her hair brushing his chin. "I know you do. It's so hard though."

Matthias stopped her there with a finger on her lips, then bowed his head as he prayed for them.

The man once more stood watching them. He was waiting for the right time. His boss wanted those two in his control, but he hadn't been able to catch them. How best to do that, he was still trying to decide. He faded back into the trees as they walked past him to Matthias' truck.

Matthias felt the truck shudder under him as he headed down the hill from the river. Not sure what was going on, he fought for control. He had nowhere he could pull over with a drop-off on either side.

"Matthias?" He could hear the fear in Larkin's voice. "What's wrong?"

"I'm not sure, Larkin. I can't tell if it's a flat tire or what. Your seat belt is tight, right?"

She nodded, her hand gripping the door handle, the other one her seatbelt. Her lips moved as she prayed.

A slow moving vehicle was suddenly in front of them. Matthias tried to slow but was unable to. To avoid the collision, he cranked the wheel to the left, hoping to slide around the vehicle, when the vehicle moved over the line into his path. Matthias gave a shout as he cranked the wheel again and slammed on the brakes. The truck shuddered and headed for the drop-off on the left. He struggled to maintain control, finally stopping just inches from the edge.

Larkin stared at him, her face white. "What happened?"

"That I don't know. How is it on your side? Can you get out?" At her nod, he pulled on the emergency brake. "Okay, open your door and drop out. Move back as far as you can. Do you hear me?" He stared at her. "Don't stay near the truck. When you get out, run. I'll be right behind you."

Matthias waited as she ran, then slowly moved over to her seat, feeling the truck edge sideways. He would only have one chance, he knew. Lord, I could use Your hand right now to pull me out of here. I don't know if I can do it on my own. Drawing it a deep breath, he dove from the truck, rolling away from it, and then on his feet, running towards Larkin. She was in his arms, tears on her face, before he had stopped moving.

A sound of metal crunching brought their heads around as Matthias' truck disappeared over the edge. He dropped to the ground, taking Larkin with him. That had been way too close!

Bill walked towards them, his head shaking at their close call. His eyes watched as the tow truck pulled Matthias' vehicle back up to the road. He stopped beside Matthias.

"What happened?"

"I have no idea. One minute, the truck was fine. The next minute I didn't have a lot of control over it." His eyes puzzled, he walked towards it, Larkin's hand tight in his. "There, Bill. See that tire? It wasn't flat earlier, and I don't think it went flat from the header it took over the side."

The tow driver spoke up. "You have a flat on this side too. Looks as if someone loosened the valve caps. But given what you say and how it felt, I would have someone go over it. There was likely something else done to it."

Matthias stared at him, then at Bill. "Really?"

Bill nodded. "They're after you now, Matthias, in order to get to Larkin. They haven't been able to get to her any other way."

Larkin paled even more at the thought and tried to tug her hand from Matthias. "Matthias, you need to leave me alone. I can't have you hurt."

"At this point, Larkin, I don't think that would make much of a difference. They'll go after whoever they can to get to you." Matthias' voice was low enough that only Bill and Larkin heard him.

"He's right, Larkin. They won't go after your family. That's not how they work. They're assuming Matthias means something to you, seeing you two together. Even if you don't go anywhere together ever again, they'll find either you or Matthias and use you one against the other. The other members of your team haven't been threatened for some reason. Nor has any of the other paramedical occupations in town. Somehow they've fixated on you, Larkin, and through you, Matthias."

Larkin's face hardened even as it paled even more. "So what do we do, Bill? I can't sit around any more waiting for the next shoe to drop or the next time they try and kill us."

"I know you can't. You both have clients tomorrow?"

"I'm booked through Thursday. I try and take Friday to do paperwork and catch up on my studies." Matthias stared into the distance, not likely what he was hearing from Bill.

"Larkin?"

"I'm booked through Friday morning. I take Wednesday afternoon to do my billing and paperwork." She stared between the two men, trying to get a feel for what they were after. "Why?"

"Because it's getting to the point where Andrew wants to shut you two away somewhere you'll be safe. At least until we get a better handle on what we're dealing with."

"That's not happening, Bill. With our occupations, we have to be with our clients each visit. It's too important to keep them going and motivated. It's not like a job you can close down the office for a while."

Bill sighed. "We know that, Matthias. What we may need to do is put you two somewhere safe and drive you to where you need to be. I have a team that's ready to do just that."

"You've done that without talking to us, Bill?" Larkin's anger came through. "That doesn't happen. I told you before. I'm part of every decision that's made."

"For now, Larkin, but there may come a time when we'll have to step in and take over."

"Not happening." Larkin stomped away, anger radiating from her.

"That went well, don't you think?" Matthias was amused at the reaction Bill got.

"Not funny, Matthias. It's life and death. Go talk some sense into your lady."

Chapter 15

Throwing his paperwork onto his desk, Matthias rose, stretched and headed for the kitchen, stopping to grab a bottle of juice from the fridge. He headed for the back deck. He was done his paperwork for the week and just needed to head back into town for groceries. He stared at the back of his yard, his eyes narrowing. Something was out of place back there. He walked from his deck and towards the back, eyes searching the area around him.

Okay, Lord, now what? He had gotten into the habit of conversing with God every day as if God was standing right there with him. What is waiting back there?

He stood, staring at the bike leaning against a tree, then searched the area around him. It wasn't his and he knew Larkin didn't have one there. He turned to face the house again, not hearing the soft whisper of sound until it was too late. The man stood over Matthias' body and looked around, before hauling Matthias to his feet and draping him over his shoulder. He headed through the field to the truck he had parked on the road back there, lowering the tailgate and dropping Matthias onto the truck bed. A few strips of duct tape and Matthias was bound and gagged. The man pulled the tonneau cover back of the truck bed and headed for the bike, shoving it into the truck as well. A few glances around, and he was behind the wheel and headed away, a cruel smile on his face. He had Matthias. Now, he would be able to get to Larkin.

Larkin stood in her doorway, her gaze fixed on Matthias' home. It was after 10 and there were no lights on, but she could see that the back door was still open. That was so unlike Matthias. He never did that. She took another look, then pulled out her phone, hunting for Bill's number. Her finger hovering over it, she paused. No, she would call Josiah. Maybe he would come.

"Josiah, hi. It's Larkin. No, I'm fine, but I think there's something wrong at

Matthias'. There are no lights on, which is really strange for him. Yes, his rental's still here. You will? Thank you. I hate to bother you and Faith."

Larkin waited for Josiah to arrive, then walks across the yard to meet him.

"No sign of him, yet?" Josiah studied her face.

"No, there hasn't been. After what we went through last Sunday, I'm afraid, Josiah. I think someone's got to him."

Josiah nodded, then pointed at the deck. "Stay right there. I'll look through the house and see if he's fallen asleep or something."

"It's the 'or something' I'm worried about, Josiah."

Thirty minutes later, the red and blue of the emergency lights flashed across her face as she watched officers search through Matthias' house and then the yard, their flashlights flickering like huge lightning bugs. Andrew and Bill stood beside her. Josiah had waited with her, then headed home with a request for them to call him when they found Matthias.

"You haven't seen him all day, is that correct?" Andrew watched the men and women of his force working the scene.

"No. I was out with clients and then with the cabinet men at my house. I didn't get home until after supper. It wasn't until after 10 that I realized something was off with Matthias." She rubbed her upper arms, suddenly chilled.

"Let's get you back into your home, Larkin, where you'll be warmer." Bill turned her and hand on her arm, led her that way. "Do you have tea?"

She looked up at him, surprised at the question. "I do. In the cabinet near the fridge."

She paced until Bill approached her and handed her a cup of tea.

"You've not likely eaten, Larkin. Drink this."

She sipped, then made a face. "It's sweetened."

"Yes, it is. Drink it." He tapped the cup.

She sipped it, making a face with each taste, until she finished it. She handed the cup back to him, and then paced more.

"Where is he, Bill?"

"We don't know, Larkin. We're looking to see what's going on."

"You're not going to find him here, Bill. I have no idea where he is, but he's not here."

An officer appeared at the door, beckoning to Bill.

"Stay put. I'll be right back. An officer is stationed right outside your door."

Bill disappeared through the door, heading for Andrew.

"Andrew?"

Andrew turned, a bleak look on his face before he nodded to the back of the yard and headed that way. "They found evidence that Matthias was likely ambushed and taken away."

"What? How?"

"That's what we don't know, Bill. It would take something big to get past him."

The crime scene tech straightened and turned to them. "It looks as if your friend was knocked out and then carried from here through the field. There's tracks of a bike being wheeled out as well, after that. There are a lot of tracks, but they're from the same boot. I've managed to get some good casts and if you find the boot, I'll be able to match it."

"Thanks, Stan. Did you follow the track?"

He shook his head. "I was about to when you two came up. Follow me and stay off to the side."

They walked to the road at the back, where Stan stopped, his light searching the ground. "There. There's some oil from a vehicle. I would say a truck by the tires." His phone out, he spoke quickly. "Lee's heading our way and will take some casts of the tread. Find me the truck and we'll match that as well."

"That's going to be like looking for a needle in a haystack. If you can figure out anything about the truck, call me." Andrew turned to walk back to the house, Bill following him.

"Andrew, what are we going to do about Larkin?"

Andrew stopped in his tracks, thoughts running through his mind. "She's not giving up her work, I can tell you that. We'll need to go through Matthias' clients and find someone who can help us with them. It's not like they can wait until he's back." He turned to face Bill, his thoughts evident. He then sighed. "Let's go talk to her. We'll need to do some work out here tomorrow when it's light. Make sure at least two officers stay put."

"Are we going to have to bring in Don and his team?"

Andrew heaved a deep sigh, then nodded. "I have a feeling we'll have to, and she's going to fight us on that. Matthias didn't disappear on his own. It's to get to Larkin and why was that? We still don't have that answer."

A week had passed, and Andrew paced his office. There had been no sign of Matthias, no ransom note, no contact, and that worried him. Don had been brought in as security for Larkin and he reported she wasn't eating much or even sleeping much. He also reported that she would sit for long periods of time watching Matthias' house, not saying anything to whoever of the team was with her. Andrew looked around at the knock on his door.

"Stan? What do you have?" Andrew pointed at a chair and seated himself behind his desk.

"Not a lot, unfortunately, Andrew. The tire treads are from a pickup, off road is what I'm told. The footprints are from a size 12 work boot. I'm sorry. I was hoping for better news."

"You've done your best, Stan. That's all I can ask."

Stan nodded as he stood. "There's been no word?" When Andrew shook his head, he continued, "I was so hoping to find something for you."

"I know, Stan. Thank you."

Andrew watched him walk away, then turned back to the reports on his desk. He was tired. No, exhausted, he thought. When would this end? How many of the friends now he thought? Four, that's it. There's still four in that group. Please, Lord, don't let this happen to all them. This is wearing out everyone. Now I know how my friend in Riverville felt when his friends when through this. This was one time he wished he had someone at home to help him chase away the darkness.

Larkin looked up as Don spoke to her. "I'm sorry, Don. I wasn't paying attention to what you're saying."

He looked at her with compassion. "It's okay, Larkin. I just asked if you needed to go anywhere or if we could get you something. Didn't you say you needed to go back to your house at some point today?"

She nodded. "Can we go now? I'd like to do it while it's still light." She shivered. "I just don't like the night anymore and that used to be my favourite time of day. Dusk, when the stars were coming out."

Don watched her with a look of compassion on his face before nodding at Paul.

Paul walked behind Don and Larkin as they approached her home. There were no trucks around now, the tradespeople having finished for the day. His eyes watchful, he stood, back to the house and looked around.

Don took her key and unlocked the door. "Wait here, Larkin. Let me go through the house first."

"Why? There have been people in and out all day. Why would there be someone here now?"

"That's what I want to make sure, that no one is still here or snuck in while they were locking up. Stay with Paul."

Don walked through the house, noting the progress. He stopped in the kitchen, his senses telling him something was off. He headed for the backdoor, then stopped, his eyes searching the room, finally stopping on the pantry. He walked over and carefully opened the door, hand on his weapon. He sighed. Not again, Lord. Not again. He pulled out his phone. Andrew would not be pleased, not at all, he thought.

He headed back to the front door, Paul turning to watch him. Don nodded at their vehicle, and Paul directed Larkin back to it, stuffing her inside and shutting the door before heading back to Don.

"What did you find?"

"Someone was in here, either as the men left or just after. They left a note in the pantry." Don watched as Larkin stared at them.

"Did you get a good look at it?"

Don nodded. "They want Larkin. Whoever it is has gotten nasty."

"That bad?" Paul's eyes searched the area around them. "How much more will she have to go through, Don? She's ready to crack now."

"I know. That worries me. Andrew's on his way and he's having a crime scene tech come out as well. We'll leave the house for them to search." He turned to Paul, a good friend as well as a team member. "This is when it's hard to remember God's in control and has a plan for us."

Andrew stood talking with Don as Paul leaned against the SUV, Larkin's window down as she watched.

"What did he find, Paul?" Her voice was quiet and subdued.

"A note, I think, Larkin. He didn't say what was on it."

She leaned her head on her arm, the breeze ruffling her hair. "Didn't he? Then I guess Andrew will have to tell me."

"I don't think he will, Larkin. Not unless it helps us to find Matthias. He'll keep it very quiet as part of the investigation. He won't tell you if it's brutal. I can guarantee you that much."

"And you think it's that bad?" She turned her head to watch him.

Not taking his eyes off the men in front of him or the activity around the house, he nodded. "I know Don. I know how he reacts. It was brutal."

Tears she refused to shed sparkled in the streetlights as they came on. "Do you think he's dead, Paul? Is that what it said?"

"We don't know that, Larkin. I don't know that. Don didn't tell me what the note said."

"And here I was so looking forward to getting back home." She studied the house she loved. "I think I'm going to have to sell it when it's finished. I don't know if I can live here again."

"It would be a shame if you can't but you may have to. Memories are brutal at times."

"You're living with yours, aren't you?"

He hesitated, then nodded. "I am, Larkin. We all are. With our line of work, we have more regrets and memories than the average person."

She nodded, watching as Don and Andrew headed her way. "Here they come, Paul. Where are they going to stick me now?"

Paul turned to her, a half-smile on his face. "And what makes you think they're going to stick you away somewhere?"

"It's what always happens in the movies and books, you know. They always stick the heroine away somewhere to keep her safe, and that never works out. The bad guys always find them."

Paul shook his head even as he laughed at her nonsense, knowing she was doing this on purpose.

Andrew's eyes flickered between the two, even as Paul shook his head at him.

"Larkin?"

"Yes, Andrew? And where are you going to hide me?"

Andrew stopped, a smile briefly crossing his face. "Who said we're going to put you somewhere?"

Paul grinned. "She just told me that's what always happens at this point in a movie. She's smart there, Andrew. I think she has your number."

Andrew shook his head, then drew his gaze back to Larkin. "Larkin?" He watched as she shuddered before looking back at him. "Don found a note in your pantry. They want to trade you for Matthias. They haven't said where he is or what shape he's in. We're not about to do that." He shot a glance at Don. "Don's going to take you back to the cottage, you'll pack your things, and go with him."

"I can't walk out on my people, Andrew, no matter what."

"We know you can't. Make a list of who you're working with, talk it over with Don, and see what you can do. Can you pass them on to anyone else?"

She shook her head. "Not all of them. It's not what we do. I have to work with them, and bringing in someone new sets back their progress."

"That's what we thought. We'll do our best to make it work, Larkin, but you need to work with us as well. Can you shorten the week at all?"

"Let me think it through and see what I can do, but with this, you need to keep to a regular schedule." She frowned, her thoughts on her clients. "There are some I'm taking to every other week. I have some new clients that I have to assess. It's not like a 9-5 job, where I can walk away and let a temp take over. That's not how an OT works."

"We get that, Larkin, but we need to keep you safe. Wherever you go, someone will be with you at all times." Don's voice was more forceful than she had heard before.

"Just what was in that note, Andrew?"

He sighed, not wanting to tell her. "They want to trade for you, like we said."

"And Matthias?   Is he even still alive?"

"We have no reason to think he isn't. We're working on that premise, Larkin."

She shook her head.   "A lot of guessing there, Andrew."

"I know, Larkin. That's what we have to do sometimes, just believe that the person is still alive until we have irrefutable proof they aren't."

Chapter 16

Matthias rolled over on the thin, dirty mattress he was lying on, tugging at the shackle fastened to the wall. It was long enough to let him roam the room somewhat, reach the facilities, but not long enough for him to reach the door or the window. He sat up, his legs stretched out in front of him on the floor, and scrubbed his hands down his face. How long had he been here? He didn't know for sure, having been unconscious for the first few hours or it could even have been days, he thought. Lord, keep Larkin safe, please. Don't let them get to her.

His eyes still bleary from the concussion he suspected he had, he closed them against the headache still raging. He finally struggled to his feet and to the bathroom, seeking relief with a cold cloth. There was a bottle of painkillers sitting on the cabinet, when it appeared he wasn't quite sure, but he refused to take any of them. He had no idea if they were still just painkillers or something else. In curiosity, he popped the top and the safety band was still in place. He stared at it, struggling to focus, before setting the bottle back down and stumbling back to the mattress, almost falling as he reached it. His eyes closing, he slid back into the black abyss he awakened from periodically.

The man stood in the doorway, watching Matthias. How hard had that fool hit him? He turned to look behind him before walking across to Matthias and nudging him with his shoe. No response. Anger rose in the man. He needed Matthias up and on his feet, alert, in the next two days or his plans were for naught. He walked from the room, locking the door behind him, his footsteps heavy with anger. Someone would pay for this, he thought, and went to find the man he knew was responsible.

Bill tracked Andrew down. "No word?"

Andrew turned from his fax machine. "Nothing. I thought we would have had more word by now. How's Larkin?"

Bill shrugged.   "She's not saying much. I talked to Don. He's going to have to leave her security to someone else soon. They have a commitment coming up they can't get out of."

"I don't like that. When?"

"Next week for a month."

Andrew sighed, his mind racing to see who they could find. "And anyone else I've contacted are tied up themselves. Anyone I would trust that is."   He turned to Bill. "Thoughts?"

"We lock her up here overnight and an off-duty officer be with her during the day."

Andrew started laughing.   "I don't think, somehow, that she'll go for that."

Bill grinned. "I already told her. Her reaction was priceless. Lily offered to stay with her overnight."

"Lily Gordon?" At Bill's nod, Andrew frowned, deep in thought.   "That would work, I think. Lily's good. See what you can arrange for off-duty officers for a couple of weeks after Don leaves. See if he has any suggestions as well."

"I already have." Bill handed over a schedule. "Here's what we have."

"Thanks, Bill. Any word at all on the investigation?"

Bill shook his head. "It's gone cold, Andrew. No one has seen or heard anything, not even our undercover officers on the street."

"That's just bizarre, Bill. Someone has to know something."

"I know. I don't get it, Andrew. It's too covered. I think we have a leak here somewhere."

Andrew's face grew stern. "I think you're likely right. Do what you need to then."

Larkin looked around her client's home, checking for anything that could trip him.

"Okay, sir. Let's get you up and to the kitchen."

He growled at her. "Not going there, young lady. You do it."

"Doesn't work that way. I'm here to help you get mobile again, not to do your work for you."

"You do what I pay you for."

She shook her head. "Sorry, you're not paying me. Your family is. Take it up with them. Now, are you going to stand up for me?"

At his refusal, she stood watching him, sighing to herself. He was a cantankerous old man, felled by a mild stroke, who had given up on life. "If you're not going to work with me, I'll have to talk to your family, you know."

"Get out. And take that other person with you."

Larkin watched him for a minute, then turned to pack up her paperwork and laptop. "I'm sorry you don't want to work with me and gain your independence again."

She walked from the room, meeting Lily at the door.

Lily looked past her and then at Larkin, before pointing to her car.

"Does that happen a lot?"

Larkin nodded. "Sometimes it does. We can't work with them if they refuse. I'll have to call the family. It will be hard for them."

"I can only imagine how hard. My Pops had a stroke and refused any help. He died about two months later. We were told that if he had worked with the therapists, he wouldn't have."

"That's so sad, Lily." Larkin sat back, her eyes watching the landscape pass by. "That was the last one for the day. Now where?"

"Home?" Lily watched as Larkin shrugged. "How be we go get some groceries? I'll cook for you tonight."

"You don't have to do that." Larkin turned to stared at her.

"I know I don't but I want to. You can finish off your paperwork, and then we'll find some sappy movie to watch. How's that?"

"Can you do that when you're on guard?"

Lily shrugged. "I can. Todd's coming over to cover for the night, so I can have a break."

"Who set this up and how many favours do I owe?"

"Bill and you don't owe any. We want to see Matthias home again and see you safe. This is our way of helping. It's your hometown, Larkin. If we can't help out someone from our town, who do we help?"

"And look who's waiting for us?" Larkin sat for a moment before she slid from the car, pulling her briefcase with her. "Now what, Bill? Come to lock me up in jail overnight?"

Bill stared at her, seeing the fatigue and stress in her face and her movements. He exchanged a look with Lily, who shook her head.

"Can we talk inside, Larkin? I don't like you outside in the open for too long, knowing Matthias was pulled from here."

Larkin pushed past him and unlocked the door, stopping as he placed a hand on her arm. "We go first, remember the drill? Larkin?"

She finally nodded and waited with Lily as Bill searched through the cottage, finally coming back to motion them in.

"Larkin, we're going to go somewhere to talk, somewhere away from here. Pack a bag. We're putting you somewhere safer than here."

"Bill, we've been through this. I can't leave my clients."

"I know you can't. I need your laptop too. I want to have it checked over."

Her eyes flew to him. "My laptop? Why?"

"Just gather what you need. Do you need anything from your office?"

She nodded. "I do. Let me do that first." She headed for the spare room she had been using as her office, Lily at her heels.

"Here's a box, Larkin. Where do you want to start?"

Larkin pointed to a pile of files. "Those are what I need for the next few weeks. Is there another box? I need to pack up forms and diagrams and client instructions as well." She stood, uncertainty in her movements.

"Larkin, let me pack up for you. You go pack some clothes." Lily's hand on her arm brought Larkin back to the room. "Bill wouldn't be doing this if he didn't fear for you."

"I know. I just hate this. Where's Matthias, Lily? Is he even still alive?" Tears she refused to shed sparkled in her eyes.

"Where's your faith, Larkin? Has God told you Matthias is dead?" When Larkin shook her head, Lily continued, "Then believe he is alive and trust God to bring him back to you. That's what our guys are working towards."

Bill turned to take the boxes from Lily and stuffed them into the back of his police SUV. He waited for Larkin to appear.

"How's she doing, Lily?"

"She's hurting, Bill, really hurting. It didn't help that today someone refused to work with her and practically threw her out of his home. She's about at her limit. I don't think she can take much more."

Bill sighed, jamming his hands into his pockets, his eyes searching the trees overhead even as he listened to the birds and insects. "I know. I hate to move her, but we have to. Even having you with her hasn't kept her totally safe."

"What do you mean?" Lily too was searching the area before turning back to Bill.

"We had a letter come in today, with a photo of Matthias. We can't tell if he's still alive, but he looks pretty rough. They still want to trade him for Larkin. Somehow they know she's still here. Did she leave you her laptop?"

Lily pointed at the boxes. "I stuck it in one of them. She'll have to work without it for a couple of days. I guess you're thinking they've remotely downloaded a program."

"That's what we're surmising. I also need her phone."

"My phone?" Larkin stood beside him. "Why?"

"Because people can hack phones and download programs that track you." Bill reached into his pocket and withdrew a phone. "Here's one you can use for now that's not traceable."

"But all my contacts are on my phone. I can't work without that."

"You'll have to for a few days, Larkin, just until we can get this sorted out." Bill pointed to the passenger door. "In. I'll explain as we go."

"What about Lily?"

"Lily's off duty for the next few days. She's been seen with you, so they'll be following her to get to you." As Larkin stood, her mouth slightly open, Bill could feel anger rising inside him. "Larkin, in the vehicle. We need to move now!"

Larkin jumped at the bite in Bill's words, then looked at Lily. Finally she moved to the door and climbed in, shutting the door carefully behind her before fastening her seatbelt. She watched as Bill and Lily shared a few more words before Bill shoved her bag into the back and shut the hatch.

Bill slid behind the wheel and watched as Lily drove away. He sighed, knowing he

had a difficult task ahead of him. How
would he get through to Larkin and still
keep her safe?

Chapter 17

*L*arkin looked around the house she had been brought to. She didn't recognize the area, having traveled from her hometown to another town. She knew Bill wanted to talk to her, but she really didn't want to hear what he had to say.

Bill stood in a doorway, watching her, knowing he had to talk to her and not knowing what her reaction would be.

"Larkin? We need to talk. Please, come sit."

She turned and finally sat in the chair he had pointed to. Bill sat across from her, just watching.

"What's going on now, Bill, that you've had to yank me from my home and work?"

Bill pulled an envelope from his pocket and turned it over and over in his hands, before pulling out a photo.

"This. We received it today at the department. We've debated whether we should show you or not. Let me say that the stakes are rising. For some reason they want you and only you. Not your work mates. Not your family. Not your friends."

"Why?"

"That's what we're not sure of, Larkin, and we need you to pick your brain. This could go back years and it likely does. The two names you gave us? We've checked them out. Both of those men are in prison. Yes, they tripped themselves up and got caught in the last five years."

Larkin's eyes slid shut. "I'm so glad they're off the streets. But why me?"

"That's what we need to figure out. I'm going to have one of our detectives and one of techs come out and work with you. We need to go back over all of your clients here in town. If we don't find anything there, then we'll be looking wider. But I think it has something to do with Elmton.

There's an undercurrent there not many people feel."

Larkin nodded. "I know. And I'm scared, Bill. Someone approached me a while ago and asked for help. I was terrified when they stopped me."

"I know they did, Larkin. An undercover officer happened to be nearby and heard it all. So they're not the ones who are after you. We need to figure out who is."

Bill stood and paced. "You brought your files?"

"Not all of them. If you can get them, we'll go through them. But I do need my laptop."

"You'll have it back tomorrow. There was a program downloaded to it that our computer tech removed and he strengthened your firewall as well. Your phone had a program too and he removed it."

"What about my family?" Bill could see the fear for them on her face.

"They're safe."

"You're sure?" At his nod, she sat back. "What am I actually looking for, Bill?"

"To tell you the truth, we're not sure. We know fraudulent billing has been done, and we're working with the insurance companies on that. They're not pressing charges against any of you and you don't have to reimburse them as the money didn't go to any of you, but to a separate account. Other than that, we'll be looking at names, accidents, injuries. Strokes may be part of it."

"That's pretty much everyone I deal with or have dealt with. Do you realize how many there are?"

"I know, Larkin. There are a lot. But we need you to concentrate on a certain age group first. Word on the street is that whoever this is has targeted someone in their 50s to 60s, that age group. Start there and then we'll work out from there."

She blew out a breath, staring at him. "Okay. It's going to take days to do this."

"I know."

Bill finally stood, walking towards the windows and drawing the drapes. "We need to keep all the windows covered, Larkin. I'm sorry."

"I'm not safe here either?"

He turned. "We're trying, Larkin, we're really trying. I have some people who will be with you over the next few days. Trained personnel. Their only task is to keep you safe. You'll work with my people and try to track back who it is. You know the town and the people. Whoever this is has hidden himself or herself well."

She nodded. "I get that, Bill. I just want this over and Matthias home safe and sound. It shouldn't have involved him."

"But it did, why at the first we don't know."

She pointed a finger at him. "That's what I can't figure out. Why was he sent to that home at the same time as me?"

Bill stopped pacing and stared at her. "That's a good question and one we haven't got an answer to yet. We're working that angle as well, searching back through Matthias' clients. Don't worry. We're doing it legally with a court order and all. He was aware of it before he disappeared and was in agreement to that.”

“Where is he, Bill?”

“I don’t know, Larkin. Somewhere close to town I would suspect. I have officers searching abandoned houses, cabins, cottages, anywhere someone could hide him.”

“But if it’s a townsperson, he could be hidden in their house in town and you wouldn’t know that.”

“We realize that, Larkin, and are working that angle. We have officers undercover as well who are working through the streets and their sources there. We’ll find him.”

“But will he still be alive?” She waved her hands to stop him from speaking. “Save the lecture. I already got it from Lily. Right now, my hope of ever seeing him again is rock bottom. It can’t get any lower. How does God deal with that, Bill? You tell me.”

“Pray, Larkin, pray hard. Tell Him exactly how you feel, every little bit of it.

He already knows but He wants to hear it from you. Here's your Bible. You hadn't packed it and Lily picked it up for you. Go. Find your prayer closet. Spend time over the next few hours with him. Don't do all the talking. Let Him talk and speak to you."

She glared at him, before taking her Bible and walking away, the bedroom door shutting harder than he expected. He sighed, his heart raised in prayer for his friend her and for Matthias.

Bill reached for his phone.

"Bill? Andrew. How's it going?"

"About how you would expect it to have gone. She's hurting, Andrew, and snapping at whoever gets in her way."

"That's what we thought would be happening. Now, how are we for personnel? Do we have enough?"

"I think so. That new security team Don hunted up for us is due in tomorrow. I'm not comfortable working with someone I don't know."

"I know. I trust Don but I've done my research on Richard's team. It's small but he's friends with Don and also Abe from Rebel's."

"He is? Then it should be okay. How many?"

"He has two men and two women, which is why Don recommended him. He thought Larkin might feel better having some women around her."

"That she should. Although she can hold her on with the men. She was asking Lily about self defense movements and Lily worked with her on some."

"She did? Good. Larkin's not sitting back and I like to hear that. Keep me updated on what you've found. I've got you covered here for the next week. Sid and Brownie are headed your way early tomorrow."

"I'll be expecting them. Tonight, we'll manage." Bill hesitated. "Andrew, we need to pray for Larkin. She said tonight her hope is all gone."

"That's what I was reading from her. We'll manage that, Bill. Any concerns, call me."

Bill pocketed his phone, then headed for the door to do his perimeter sweep. He was on his own that night and felt uncomfortable. How did it get to this point, Lord?

Larkin looked up the next morning as she heard footsteps approaching the kitchen. Bill appeared, followed by a man she didn't know.

"Larkin, this is Richard. Don's a friend of his and asked him to step in for him on your security."

"More security?" She sighed as she studied both Bill and the man standing behind him. "Hello, Richard. There's coffee, tea, or cold drinks in the fridge. Help yourself."

Richard shared an amused look with Bill before moving to grab a mug and make himself a tea. "You have quite the selection of teas here, Bill."

"I know. I don't know who stocked us up with supplies, but they grabbed just about something of everything."

Richard turned to lean against the counter, one hand grabbing the edge, the other holding his mug of tea.

"Larkin, can we talk?"

She threw her pen down and looked up at him. "That's all I seem to do lately, is talk to someone new."

"I'm sorry about that. I know how hard that can be." He watched as her eyes found his. "We need to talk to you, to find out what we can do to keep you safe. I have two men and two ladies on my team. We're often called in to watch out for ladies in distress. Just for your information, Don's a good friend of mine. We grew up together, side by side houses in fact."

"You did?" She glanced between Bill and Richard. "So what do you need to know?"

"First, do you need to visit any of your clients in the next few days? Do you need to pick up any material, do any shopping?"

She sat back, staring at him. "I'm not going to be kept a prisoner?"

Richard laughed. "Not really. We work with our clients, trying to keep their life as normal as possible. If we can't, then we work with them to keep them as safe as possible. I need a schedule from you, first. Then I go over it and we decide from there where and what you do."

She sighed. "I'm a prisoner. Just under a different name."

Richard broke out in laughter as Bill stared at her. "I like your humour, Larkin. That will get you through a lot. Now, you're in the middle of your breakfast. Bill and I are going to do a walkthrough of what we have here. Then he's heading for town to find Andrew."

"Bill, have you any word this morning?" Larkin's eyes were hopeful.

"I'm sorry, Larkin. Not since we got that photo and note yesterday. I know. I didn't show you the photo and I'm not about to. You don't need to see it. Suffice it to say, Matthias is still alive."

Richard spoke up. "My experience has been that he will stay alive as long as they need him. We'll make them need him a long time, enough time to find out who they are and find out where he is."

Larkin looked down at the piece of toast she had been eating and pushed her plate away. "I'm not hungry any more. Where do you want me to set up, Bill?"

"How about the dining room? We've extended the table so you can spread out your work. I put the boxes you brought in there. Sid and Brownie stopped and picked up the rest for you. They'll be here shortly."

"And how do you know they weren't followed?"

Bill spun around to look at her. "Good question, Larkin. We've taken precautions. This is an isolated spot, with only one way in and out. I have someone posted at the end of the road with roadblocks and no one who isn't on the list gets through."

"Does it really work like that?" Larkin was curious. "Does it really stop someone who wants through?"

"It should. The forest around here is overgrown with just game trails through it. I know the people who own it. No one gets close to the house without us knowing."

She nodded before rising and placing her plate into the sink. She'd wash it later.

First she needed to head for the dining room. She hesitated and instead headed for the room she had spent the night in and reached for her Bible, needing to find some promises of God that would calm her and give her hope.

Richard watched her walk away, then turned to Bill. "She's hurting in more ways than one, Bill."

"She is, Richard, and I have no idea how to help her."

Richard nodded. "It's good to know how she's feeling. It's when they hide their feelings and cover up, that's when it's hard to protect them. They become unpredictable."

"Trust me. You'll know exactly how Larkin feels. She tells you, in a nice way, but leaves no doubt in your mind how she's doing."

Chapter 18

*T*wo days later, Larkin sat back, eyes on her laptop. She had been making notes, taking down names. Brownie she knew had made up a spreadsheet with the information she had thrown at him. Something was missing, and she wasn't sure what.

Richard watched from the doorway, his head turning as he heard the door open and Naomi, one of his team, walked in.

"How are they doing, Richard?" Naomi's voice was low.

"They've made progress but I can see Larkin is frustrated. She needs to take it off the computer and spread it out somehow."

"There are rolls of paper in the SUV we had on hand. Stephen threw them in, I have no idea why."

"Good man. He's learning how to think outside the box, isn't he?"

Naomi laughed. "You've taught us well, Richard. I'll go get some. I'm sure he threw in markers and tape as well."

"Thanks, Naomi. Send Stephen in with it and I'll help him get it on the walls. I need you to stay close to Larkin. She's about ready to break, she's that brittle."

"She is, Richard. She denies there's anything between them, but I know she has feelings for Matthias. I don't think she's even thought about how deep they run."

"No, I don't expect she has."

Larkin watched as Richard and Stephen tacked pieces of paper on the wall, a frown in place. Now what were they up to?

Richard turned to find Larkin watching him. "Larkin, we don't have white boards for you three to work on. I can see the frustration you're feeling. Play detective for me. What you're doing on your laptop, transfer to here if you can. That way we can all work on it for you." He held up a hand at her protest. "We've gotten judicial clearance and the proper warrants to do this. You have a judge in town on your side."

"I do? Who?"

"Judge Foxcroft. I understand he's good friends with your dad."

"He is. They've been friends since high school. Wow! Friends in high places, huh?" She sat back and watched as Sid and Brownie moved towards the wall. "I think it will take more than one wall, though, Richard."

He laughed as he pointed at Stephen. "That's why he's in here right now. We'll put up the paper and leave you three to work it."

"Richard, when you're done, can you stay? Maybe you'll see something one of us doesn't, given your line of work."

"I can do that. I'll let you three get started and then come back."

Larkin watched him walk away, then turned back to her laptop. "So, how do we do this? I've never done this before."

Sid laughed. "Not a problem, Larkin. First, let's list all the names in a separate column. Then, we'll list their ailments. Then, how you were contacted and by whom. Then we'll just keep adding all that information we've dug up."

"Do you think this will work?"

Brownie spoke up. "It's worth a try, Larkin. I know we have a spreadsheet working, but good old-fashioned marker and paper can sometimes trigger a thought or show a connection we don't see."

Four hours later, Richard called a halt. "Let's take a break. Naomi's got sandwiches ready for us. Leave this for about an hour while we eat and then come back. It may be you'll see something when you've stepped back."

Larkin nodded, a frown on her face as she stared at the three walls covered in paper. "All I see is a mess right now"

"That's no way to talk about our work!" Brownie explained in mock anger. "We've done good, Larkin. You know your clients well and that helps."

Larkin nodded and turned to the kitchen, stopping suddenly before spinning around to stare at the wall, her eyes searching for a name. Her eyes slid closed as she found it. The men watched as she walked towards the wall, Naomi appearing in the doorway to call them for lunch.

Larkin stared at the name and then read the information underneath it. No wonder Eve had come to work for them. No wonder the men from the town were so concerned. She reached for a marker, circling the name, before turning around.

"This is the one, guys. This one all along. Why didn't I see it?"

Richard reached to steady her, having followed her across the room. "Come out and sit with us, Larkin. Eat if you can, but at least get some liquid into you. Set this aside for now. We'll come back in here in an hour. I promise."

She nodded as she searched his face, trusting he would do what he said.

The next day, Andrew looked up as Bill tapped at his door, then motioned him in and for him to shut the door.

"Where do we stand now, Bill?" He watched Bill sink into one of his chairs, fatigue evident.

"Larkin's memory of her clients is amazing. I can't remember that much about who I've dealt with, but she can really remember some. That name she gave us?" At Andrew's nod, he continued, "I've tracked it. Not the top player but certainly one of them. We're searching land records now for houses and properties attached to it. If God wills, we'll find Matthias soon."

"I hope we do. I understand Larkin's not eating."

"We're making her. Richard is good. He refuses to let her do anything if she won't eat. And Naomi's a great cook."

"That's good news. She had lost quite a bit of weight the last time I saw her."

"She has, but we're working on that. Any word from the streets as to where Matthias is?"

"No and that's frustrating in itself."

"It's strange how he just disappeared into thin air."

"I know. I don't like it. And we haven't had any for from those men again. They would find a way to contact Larkin if they needed to." Andrew stood, a thought crossing his mind. "Bill, head for Matthias' and check her cottage. I'm heading to her home. Meet me back here when you're done. We've been concentrating on keeping her safe and forgetting they may have put a letter at either place."

Bill headed for the door. "I'll check her office as well."

Andrew stood in front of Larkin's house, eyes searching. There were still trades people working inside, he knew. He headed for the door, stopping to look around the front porch and into the mailbox. Empty.

Walking into her home, he looked around, impressed with the colours and wood flooring she had chosen. It was a home, not a house. He walked through to the kitchen, stopping to speak with the carpenter working that day, who pointed at the kitchen counter.

His heart dropping, Andrew walked toward the counter, eyeing the mail sitting there. He flipped through it before he gathered it up and took it with him. There was a letter there, just as he thought. How long had it been there, Lord, and did their oversight mean Matthias' death?

Bill took one look at Andrew's face and sank into the chair. He hadn't found anything, but obviously Andrew had.

"You found it?"

Andrew nodded. "I just hope Matthias is still alive. I have no idea when this came. The workers have been putting the mail on the counter for her." Andrew stopped speaking and looked up at Bill. "You know, anyone could have walked in and out of that house with no one being the wiser."

Bill sat back, his thoughts racing. "We'll have to go through the house before she moves back, just in case."

Andrew agreed. "How did we miss that?"

"I don't know, Andrew, but somehow we did, trying to keep her safe, looking for Matthias, on top of everything else we are dealing with. Crime is up for some reason."

"What does it say?" Bill pointed at the letter Andrew held.

Andrew drew a deep breath and opened it, scanning it. "About the same as the last three, giving her twenty-four hours to meet them or Matthias is dead. But they don't give a meeting place or any way to contact them."

"That's bizarre, you know. How's she to contact them?"

"I know. That doesn't make sense, now does it? Unless they're watching her every move and plan on snatching her when she's out and about."

"That's more like it." Bill sighed. "At least, I hope we have her safe. Richard says she's still adamant about going to her clients, and he's trying to come up with a compromise about that."

"I hope he can. She won't be satisfied until she's back with her people."

Bill nodded as he rose. "Let me take that to the lab and see what they can come up with. Likely nothing, but we'll see."

Richard watched as Larkin sat curled up in the corner of the couch, notepad on her knee, pen in hand. He frowned. She had been sitting like that for the past twenty minutes.

"Larkin?" He approached and sat down beside her.

She shook her head and then looked at him. "Richard? Did you need something?"

"No. I just wanted to make sure everything was all right with you."

"No, it's not, but it's not your fault." She stared down at her notepad. "I'm trying to think of other names that might be the ones but so far all I can think of is Matthias, wondering how he is."

"I know it's hard, Larkin, but we don't know anything yet about Matthias. Keep trusting he's fine."

"And how do I do that, Richard? God never hears my prayers or answers me, at least not any more. He hasn't since I was a teen."

"And why is that? What hasn't He answered?"

She shook her head, not willing to bare her soul to someone almost a stranger. "Just everything, I guess."

"Sounds to me you're running and running as hard as you can from God. Turn and run towards Him, Larkin. Run to that strong tower He is.”

“Do you do that?”

Richard nodded. “I’ve had to learn to do that, Larkin. It’s not something that’s innate in us. We have to learn to trust, to believe in Someone we can’t see. We need to trust that He is who He says He is. We need to experience the safety of that strong tower, to let Him have control.” He pointed at her. “That’s the hardest part, letting go of control. It’s not our nature to do that, now is it?”

She shook her head. “No, it’s not, and that scares me.”

“Tell Him that.”

“What? I can’t talk to Him like that!” Larkin was shocked.

“Yes you can. How do you talk to your Dad, formally or as a daughter who loves her Daddy deeply? God is our Abba Father, which in loose translation means Daddy. He delights to hear His children’s voices as they talk to Him. Formality isn’t necessary, as long as we remember who He is. I’ve screamed at Him, gotten mad, cried, yelled, and then sat and listened in the silence of who He is. He speaks in different ways to different people."

"That sounds too easy." Larkin had a spark of hope in her eyes, the first Richard had seen.

He reached out his hand, palm up. She looked at him, then took his hand, watching as his head bowed.

"Father, I have a friend here who is hurting so badly she can't express what or how. You know exactly what it is and what she needs at this moment. Help her to see You as her beloved Father, the one who wants the best for her. Help her to trust. Give the hope that is crushed within her back to her once more. Help her to listen with her heart, not her head. Thank you, Father. Love You."

Larkin had stared at Richard and caught his eye as he raised his head. He smiled. "It's that simple, Larkin. It may only be a few words at the first, but talk to Him. Tell Him how you feel, where you're at and what you need. Tell Him you love Him. He always wants to hear that."

She nodded as he rose and walked away. She sat for a few minutes, then dropping the notepad and pen on the coffee table, headed for her room and solitude. Would it really work, she wondered? She had messed up everything so badly so far.

Richard stood and watched her walk to her room, his head turning as he heard Naomi approaching him.

"Gave her the 'talk', did you?" Naomi was familiar with Richard and how he addressed God.

"I did, Naomi. She needed it. She's hurting and just not from this. Until she can let go of that, she'll be stuck in the same place she is for the rest of her life."

"That she will be, Richard. Are you sure you're not a minister with a gun?"

Richard laughed as he turned for the kitchen. "No, I'm not, but we are called to minister and encourage. Sometimes that ministry calls for tough love."

"It does. I've seen you do this so many times, but I can't imagine me doing something like that."

"It's not who you are, Naomi. Your gift is hospitality, not this. But you are an encourager in your own way."

"Thank you, Richard. Now, what can I get you?"

"I'm good, Naomi. Joseph and Lynn have the night shift. Head for bed. I'll be gone early in the morning. I need to meet with Andrew."

Chapter 19

Matthias slouched against the wall, sitting on the thin mattress. His vision had cleared and his headache was better, but he still had attacks of vertigo. Not what he wanted. How was he ever to get out of here? He reached for the bolt holding his shackle and pulled. It just moved, didn't it, he thought? Shooting a glance at the door, he pulled again. Yes, it had moved.

Then he slumped back. What good would it do if he did manage to get the bolt out? He could tell he was on the second floor of a house and he had heard the door locked each time it was closed. He stared at the door, wondering how he could ever get away. From the little he had overheard, the men couldn't find Larkin, and if they couldn't find her, then they couldn't get to her. He knew it was only a matter of time before they decided he was dead weight and got rid of him.

He didn't look up as the door opened and he heard the man enter. He refused to talk to him, instead keeping his eyes on the floor.

This time, he didn't get away with it. A sudden blow sent him spinning away from the mattress, the shackle tightening on his arm.

"Where is she?"

Matthias shook his head. "I don't know. I don't even know what day it is, so how would I know where she is?"

The kick to the ribs took his breath. "You have to know."

"I don't. I don't know her well enough to know what her full schedule's like."

The man stood over him, watching before he finally walked away, the door closing behind him.

Matthias finally rolled over, hand to his ribs. His eyes were on the door. He hadn't heard it lock, had it? Was that a trick or a test they were putting his way? Or Lord is it like You have Your hand here, letting me get away?

Matthias pulled at the bolt, frantically working it loose. He searched and found his jacket, shoving his arms into it, and gathering up the shackle to use as a weapon. He crept for the door and turned the knob. The door opened, and he waited. Stepping through, he crept to the back stairs, waiting, listening. He could hear voices from the front of the house and prayed no one was in the back part. He peeked around the corner, then headed for the door, praying it didn't squeak as he opened it. It was dark, and there were no motions sensors there. He looked around. He was in town after all. Not quite sure where he was, he crept along the back of the house and headed for an alleyway he could see.

Praying he could get away, he stumbled down the alley, not sure where he was heading, other than he was heading away from the house. He didn't see a dark form rise from ahead of him, wait and then follow.

At the end of his strength, he stopped, leaning on the rough brick wall of a building. He started as a voice spoke beside him.

"Are you all right, man? You look a little shaky on your feet. Come with me. I'll get you out of here. You're running from someone."

Matthias squinted at the man, who was unkempt and appeared unclean. He finally nodded, unable to speak.

The man's arm slipped around him as he pulled Matthias' arm over his shoulder and headed towards the centre of town, finally stopping at the door of an empty building. He pulled it open and hauled Matthias into it, finally settling him on his own pallet of rough blankets. Matthias' eyes slid closed, he couldn't stop them.

The man stood watching, then reached for the shackles. A quick twist with a wire he pulled from his pocket and the bonds dropped away. He gathered them and set them aside, reaching for Matthias' wrist to scan it. It was red and raw, but he didn't have anything to treat it with.

The man finally rose, knowing Matthias would be out for a bit, and headed for the door. He found a payphone and made a call, then turned to the small convenience store behind him. He drew out his change, not looking at the clerk as he paid for his few purchases. The clerk looked around, then handed him back the money, telling him to get himself a meal.

He nodded, then looking around quickly, headed back for Matthias. He had bandages for his wrist and food and water for him.

Andrew looked up at a knock at his door and Bill entered, suppressed energy coming from him.

"Matthias is free. I got word just now from one of our undercover men. He found him and has him where he crashes."

Andrew sat back. "Now, that's good news. Are you heading out to get him?"

"Not tonight. I'm told Matthias was roughed up pretty good and our man thought I should wait until tomorrow. I'll stage it somehow that it doesn't look as if he was turned in."

"Sure, not a problem. Sounds like a plan. Now, does our man know where he was held?"

"He does and gave me the address. It's in the downtown area, not where we were looking. I have someone running a search to find the owner.”

“We’ll need to let Larkin know once we have Matthias to safety. I’d like to get the two of them together if I can.”

“I’ll head out to talk to Richard. No, on second thought, I’d better just call him. I don’t want to make too many trips his way if I can help it.”

“Sounds good. Keep me updated.” Andrew scanned his desk. “I’m going to be here all night by the looks of this paperwork.”

“You’re burning out, Andrew. Have you decided yet if you’ll take the chief’s position?”

Andrew sat back. “I’m still praying about it, Bill. I’m not sure. I’ll be heading out for some time off in about three weeks. I’m planning on making it a matter of real prayer at that point.”

“I think you should. I know you enjoy your work with the county, but this town has your heart.”

Andrew watched as Bill walked away, knowing he was right. If only, Lord, I had a lady, maybe it would make it easier to decide. I'd have someone to talk it over with, rather than a friend, one who it really mattered to.

Richard thoughtfully tucked his phone back into his pocket the next morning. It was good news for a change. He looked around for his team, motioning them to gather outside.

"Richard?" Stephen spoke. "You have news, and not bad news by the look on your face."

"It's good news. Bill is heading out shortly to pick up Matthias. Somehow he managed to get away from his captors and he's safe for now. What we need to do is plan to get Matthias and Larkin back together and keep them safe. I think we're going to need to move from here. Naomi, I'll let you get her ready to move. Nothing but clothes and her Bible go with her. Stephen, if you can pack up the dining room and have it ready for Bill's people to pick up."

"We can do that." Naomi shared a look with Stephen. "Where are we heading?"

"I'm waiting to hear back from Bill. We'll pick up Matthias, get him checked out by a physician, and then stick them away somewhere safe."

Bill watched from the shadows as Matthias was hurried out of the building, stumbling as he walked, in the predawn light. He searched the area, but could see no watchers. His eyes lifting, he saw what he assumed was a homeless man watching, frowning as he caught the man's eyes. Then, his face cleared. It was him. Now he knew who the rescuer was. He would make sure he was commended, albeit quietly.

His attention turned to Matthias as he was shoved down on the front seat of Bill's car, his head lolling on the seat back. He walked towards the officers, then slid behind the wheel, heading away from the downtown and then from the town itself. He sent a single text message, then shut his phone off and stuck in back into his pocket. This was the tricky part, getting Matthias and Larkin back together. He had to go on his own. It was be a giveaway if too many men or vehicles left the scene.

He paused at the road leading to the safe house, his eyes searching behind him, and just waited. He finally turned in to head for the house, stopping as a man stepped in front of him. A few quiet words and he headed up the lane. Stopping near the other vehicles, he turned to Matthias. Matthias had not moved since he was pushed into the car. Bill could see the pain and rough treatment on Matthias' face, the weight loss. He slid from the car as Richard and Stephen approached.

"Bill?" Richard's voice was low.

"I have him, Richard, but he's in rough shape. He looks like he was roughed up last night. I have no idea, other than God, how he managed to get away."

"Doesn't matter, as long as he's free. Let's get him into the house. Stephen here has paramedic training, so we'll let him look him over. Larkin's still sleeping. I hope she does until we can get Matthias assessed."

Bill stood back from the bed beside Richard as Stephen worked over Matthias.

"He's got a concussion, I would say, Richard. Not to mention the bruised ribs. Someone kicked here pretty good. I don't think they're fractured, just bruised. We'll have to watch that. He's had a good blow to the face as well. Almost hard enough to break his jaw."

"Is it broken?" Bill spoke quietly, his eyes shifting to the closed door.

"No. It's bruised good. We'll need to get some ice on it. I'm more concerned about the head injury. I would think it's probably not the first one he's had in the last couple of weeks."

"Why would you say that?" Richard moved closer as Stephen pointed.

"That. There's a large fading bruise on the side of his head. That didn't happen yesterday. It likely happened when he was taken and it looks as if it was with a pretty heavy object. I don't feel there's been a fracture, but he should have an X-Ray or CT scan to make sure."

"And how do we do that without causing a stir?"

"I have a friend who owns his own X-Ray, ultrasound and CT facility. If we need to, he'll help us."

"Keep it in mind if we need to." Richard headed for the door. "Bill, we need to get you out of here before Larkin sees you. Stephen, can you clean Matthias up as best you can? He looks about your size. Do you have some extra clothes you can lend him until we get him more?"

Bill spoke up. "No need. I slipped into his house last night and packed a bag for him. I'll leave it with you."

Larkin looked around as Richard approached her. "What's going on, Richard? There was a lot of commotion earlier."

"We're moving today, Larkin. I need you to only take your bag with your clothes and your Bible. Everything else stays here. Bill's people will pick it up."

She shook her head. "I can't. I have clients to see."

"Not this week. I've spoken with each family, let them know you were unavailable and found someone I trust to step in for you. Not one of your friends from the office."

Larkin looked at him, anger brewing beneath the surface. "You've taken a lot on yourself, Richard."

"Yes, I have. It's called keeping you alive. Now, finish up. I want to be on the road in fifteen minutes."

Larkin stood, looking down at her unfinished breakfast. "Something happened overnight, didn't it, Richard? And where are the rest of the team? I see you and Naomi, no one else."

"They've gone ahead. Now move. When I tell you to move and you have only some many minutes, I mean it. If you're not packed in that length of time, we still leave."

She flew to her room. Thankfully, she hadn't unpacked, so it was only a matter of a minute or two to stick what she had out into her bag. Lord, I have no idea where we're heading, but You do. Lead us.

Richard nodded as she appeared in front of him. "Naomi, you ready? Okay, then let's roll."

Larkin watched from the backseat as Richard headed back towards Elmton and then drove through heading for the other side of town. Out into the country, he finally pulled off onto a narrow dirt road, stopping in front of a small house set well back from the road.

"This is it?"

"It is." Richard shared a look with Naomi, before turning to look at her. "You asked if something happened overnight. It did. Your fellow somehow got away and got to help. Bill brought him out before dawn and Stephen looked him over." He watched as her eyes slid closed and tears trickled out from below her eyelids. "He's been hurt, Larkin. Stephen thinks he has a concussion as well as some bruising. I'll take you to him, but you need to understand that right now, he's unconscious. I heard from Stephen a bit ago. He's got him settled here. If we need to seek treatment for him, we will."

Larkin nodded, then in a quiet voice, quiet enough he could barely hear her, she spoke, "Please take me to him. I need to see him."

"We will. Just know that if we need to move again, we won't move the two of you together. If we have to separate you two, we will. Don's aware of what's happening, and he's ready to spring two of him men to come back here and work with us."

She nodded and reached for the door. "Please, Richard?"

He nodded and came around to open her door. "Work with us, Larkin. I know you want to see your clients, but we have that handled for now. Naomi here will be with you still. The rest of the team is as well. Matthias will be Stephen's charge. He'll take you in to see him as soon as he can."

Larkin stood waiting, her arms wrapped around her, watching the door behind which Matthias lay. Thank you, Lord, for bringing him back to me. Heal him.

Stephen stood in the open doorway and studied Larkin, before stepping aside. He stopped her with a hand on her arm.

"He's still out of it, Larkin. I don't know how long he will be. I'm thinking he's had a couple of concussions lately, which makes this concerning. You can stay with him for a while, but you need to leave if I say you have to. I'll be back in a few minutes with some ice packs for his face."

Her eyes lifted to him, a frown in place, before she moved past him. She stopped, hand to her mouth, as she stared at his battered face. Stephen watched in compassion before pulling the door shut, standing against it, his head leaning back on it. He was worried, to say the least, knowing how concussions could be so serious.

Larkin dropped to her knees beside the bed, her hand going to touch Matthias' face before she reached for his hand, gripping it tightly. She listened as he moaned slightly, his head moving from side to side. Lord, heal him, please. I don't think I could take it if he doesn't make it.

Chapter 20

*A*ndrew went looking for Bill, not knowing if he was in the building. He found him in the evidence room, searching through past cases.

"Bill? What are you doing?" Andrew was puzzled.

"I found a link to an old case, Andrew, and I wanted to see the evidence. It's one we never solved." He found the boxes he needed and pulled them forward, before signing them out and heading back to the boardroom.

"What case?"

"You remember that hit and run where the young female was killed walking near the county border and we had to share investigation with the town force?"

"I do.   They couldn't solve it and refused to share their evidence with us. Why that one?"

"Something about what Larkin's been going through has bugged me and last night while I was waiting to go get Matthias, I remembered it.   There's something similar to it and I needed to search through it."

"What can I do to help?"   Andrew reached for one of the boxes.   "Did you get our friend with his friend?"

"I did.   They're concerned about his health but are looking after him.   They've moved them again."

"Good.   Now, about this cold case. What exactly are you looking for?"

"I'm really not sure, Andrew. I'll have to go through it all until I figure it out."   Bill turned as he heard footsteps stop at the door. "Brownie? What brings you by?"

"Nothing really. I guess I'm grasping at straws, but I wanted to talk to you about a cold case."

Bill pointed at the door. "Come in and shut the door. Now, what case?"

"The Forrester one."

Bill shot a glance at Andrew before he spoke. "Now, that's interesting. Guess what evidence and case files I have here?"

"Really? Okay, where do I start?"

Matthias stirred, his eyes flickering open and closed. His head pounding, he tried not to move, knowing it would make it worse. He felt hands under his head raising it enough so that he could drink. He swallowed the tablets placed in his mouth, not caring any more if they were poison or not. He sighed, drifting back into blackness, sure he heard Larkin calling his name.

Larkin knelt by his bedside, her voice pleading with him to wake up. Stephen straightened up from where he had bent over Matthias and set the glass on the bedside table, his eyes watchful. He stepped away as he heard Richard stop in the doorway.

"How is he?" Richard kept his voice low, his eyes on Larkin.

"He was awake for a few seconds, but he's in a lot of pain. I managed to get some more painkillers down him. I don't know, Richard. I don't like this."

"I know. Neither do I but we can't chance him being in the hospital unless you feel it's really necessary."

"Give me a couple of more hours. I'm going to keep trying to rouse him. If by midnight, I can't, then I suggest I head in to Doc Hedley's."

Richard nodded. "Why don't I head out and bring him here? He's worked with us before so he's familiar with the routine."

Stephen nodded. "I would like that. I'm limited in what I can do for him. Larkin's about had enough, but I can't get her to leave him."

"See if you can get something down her. Try a sedative in it."

"That's what I was thinking, Richard. I hate to do it but we need to get her out of there and to her bed."

"I'll leave it with you. I'll head out for Doc."

Stephen had gotten a cold juice down Larkin and now waited, watching as she grew drowsy. He knew she'd be upset but they didn't have much of a choice. She refused to leave Matthias' side and they needed her to. He finally gathered her up in his arms and headed for her bedroom, Naomi on his heels. A few quiet words and Stephen shut the door behind him, just as Richard walked back in with Doc.

"Doc. Good to see you, even under these circumstances."

"I hear you have a patient for me." Doc was prematurely gray, but Richard's team knew he would help them in any way he could.

"In here. I guess Richard's filled you in on what happened?"

Doc nodded as he stood watching Matthias. "Have you gotten any pain meds down?"

"A couple of Tylenol about three hours ago. I doubt he's had anything else."

"Not likely. Okay, Stephen, it's you and me again. Richard, I'll be out when I'm done. But first, where's the lady?"

Stephen smiled. "I got a sedative down her in some juice and she's sleeping."

"Did you? She's not going to speak to you in the morning."

Stephen gave a low laugh. "I'm not worried. You taking care of Matthias will change that. Naomi's with her. You may want to give a look at her when you're done with Matthias."

Doc finally straightened. "Your assessment is bang on again, Stephen. Sure you're not an MD? Concussion, at least two, in the last couple of weeks. Bruising. The ribs are really bruised. He took a good kick here, didn't he?" Doc bent back over the area. "Do you have a camera that has good close up? There's something there."

Stephen watched as Doc took his photos, then stepped back beside him.

"See? There's some kind of writing. I'm surprised his ribs didn't break if that's how hard they kicked him."

Stephen reached for the camera and studied the photo. "You're right. I'll have Richard pass this on to Bill and Andrew. Surely their team can clean up the photo enough to identify it."

Doc stood watching Matthias. "I think if you continue as you are, waking him up if you can every couple of hours, you'll do fine. Don't hesitate to have Richard come for me. I would stay with what you're doing for pain meds. I've brought some IVs and whatnot for you. If he hasn't been eating, we need to get him re-hydrated."

Stephen reached to shake Doc's hand. "Thanks so much, Doc. We appreciate it."

"Listen, your team helped me out years ago. It's my turn to pay back."

Stephen turned to watch him leave, then reached for the IV needle. Doc was right. He needed to start an IV.

Larkin stretched the next morning, feeling rested but a bit groggy. Then her eyes flew open and she rose, staring down at her clothes. She hadn't got to bed properly last night, she thought. That's strange. She reached for clean clothes, then headed to the bathroom to shower and change. Refreshed she headed next for the kitchen, stopping in the doorway as she saw Richard.

"Richard?"

"Did you sleep last night, Larkin?"

"Richard, what did you do?"

"Stephen gave you a sedative." He raised his hand as she went to protest. "It wasn't done lightly, Larkin. You needed your sleep and there was no way you were heading for bed with Matthias down the hall from you."

Larkin spun, staring behind her. "Matthias?" As she moved to walk towards his door, her arm was grasped lightly by Richard.

"Come, sit down, and eat something. Naomi's made some scrambled eggs and toast." At her protest, his voice grew stern. "If you do not eat, I will not let you into Matthias' room to see how he is this morning. You will be kept out and only get reports twice a day." He stared at her as she spun to watch him. "This is how it works, Larkin. You eat and keep your strength up. You sleep and get rested. I have no idea what the future will hold, and we need to get you back to where you should be. Your fighting us on this will not help either one of you."

Larkin glared at him, then sat, accepting the food put in front of her with a quiet thanks. Naomi shared a looked with Richard before he walked from the room.

"It's hard, I know, Larkin, but Richard really does have your safety in mind when he says this." Naomi sat across from Larkin.

"I know," Larkin sighed, "but it's so hard. How is Matthias?"

"I haven't heard this morning, but I think he's okay. You'll need to talk to Stephen." When Larkin looked at her, she continued, "Stephen's our paramedic, fully trained and all."

"I didn't realize that."

"He is. And they brought in a friend last night who's a physician to check him out. No, it's okay. He agrees to be blindfolded and never gives away anything."

"That's good." Larkin pushed back her plate. "I've had enough. It was delicious."

Naomi rose, looking behind Larkin, who turned. Richard stood in the doorway, his eyes on Larkin, an unreadable look on his face.

"Come with me, Larkin. Matthias is still unconscious but he is rousing some.

Stephen's been with him overnight. Just so you know, he's battered and bruised, looking worse than he did when you saw him last night."

"I expected nothing less. Can I please see him?"

Richard took her hand and led her to the bedroom next to hers. "He's in here. I know you'll want to stay with him all day, but we can't let you do that. We'll give you some time with him every couple of hours. That's the best we can do, Larkin. He needs to rest and recover."

She nodded, her eyes glued to the door. She hesitated when it opened and Stephen emerged, standing aside to let her enter. She searched his face, taking hope at his smile.

Crossing the threshold, she hesitated once more before crossing to the bed, dropping her knees beside it. She reached out a hand to touch Matthias' face, then grasped his hand in hers, silent tears streaking down her face.

Richard watched for a few minutes, then nodding to Stephen, walked away. He headed outside, needing to touch base with

Andrew and find out how long they would need to be here. He had a feeling things were coming to a head, but he still had a task to do.

Larkin reluctantly arose when Stephen came back for her.

"He's rousing bit by bit, Larkin. Doc says he'll likely be awake in the next day or so."

"Is he okay, though, Stephen?"

"Doc wants to assess him once he's awake again, but that won't be for a couple of days. I'm praying we get to stay here for a few days to let that happen."

Larkin sighed. "In other words, you could pack us up today and move us and that would go bad for Matthias."

"That's it in a nutshell, Larkin. We need to keep him as still as we can for the next couple of days. I can see he's settled down more since you've been in there. I'll come get you in another hour or so."

Stephen stepped back into the room and shut the door, closing Larkin away from the man she now knew she cared deeply for. She paced, not settling down to anything for the next while, then sighing to herself, sat and reached for her notepad and pen. She still wasn't comfortable with just that name and started tracing his family. Naomi came and sat beside her, watching what she was doing.

"What are you hoping to track, Larkin?"

Larkin looked up quickly, startled to see Naomi sitting there. "I didn't hear you come in, Naomi. What I hope to do is trace his family. He's been an institution in town for years, for as long as I can remember I think." She studied her notes, then pointed. "See this name? She married into the family, but I always heard her family just skirted the legal side of anything. The same with this one, and this one."

Naomi reached for the notepad. "You've done a lot of work here, Larkin. Sure you're not a detective?" She grinned at Larkin's look. "Can I have these sheets? I want to give them to Richard."

Larkin shrugged. "If you think it will do any good, you can. It's more just random notes and thoughts. I haven't connected them to anything."

"It doesn't matter if you have or haven't, Larkin. One of these names may be the key Bill and Andrew are looking for." Naomi looked towards the hall. "Stephen's looking for you again, I think. Before you go, though, Larkin, just know we're all praying for you both."

Larkin turned to her. "Thank you. I don't know if anyone has ever said that out loud to me before."

Stunned, Naomi watched her walk away, then rouse to find Richard.

"Richard?" He turned as she approached, puzzled at the troubled look on her face. "Do you know what Larkin just said to me? She told me that no one had ever told her they're praying for her, not out loud."

Richard stared at Naomi, then back at the house. "That's not the way it should be, Naomi. Thank you. Now, what do you have in your hand?"

She looked down at the sheets of paper. "Larkin's been working. Here. She's drawn up as many names as she can think of who are connected to the other name."

"Really? Guess that's what happens when you live and work in a small town." He studied the names. "Did she point out anyone in particular?"

Naomi pointed out the names Larkin had mentioned, and Richard circled them. "I'll get this to Bill or Andrew. Hopefully, it will help. Bill's from the town, but Andrew isn't, so Bill may have more insight into than even Larkin." He turned to face the house. "How is she really doing?"

Naomi shrugged as she stared into the distance. "I can't read her, Richard, and that's so unusual for me. She's buried something so deep I don't think she'll ever bring it up. It's affecting her relationships with everyone though. I have seen a change in her somewhat. She's loosening up some. Whatever you said to her the other day seemed to help."

"And having Matthias here with her will help as well. Did Stephen say how he is?"

"I haven't talked to him since this morning, but he's heading our way. I'll catch up with you later."

"Richard, can we talk?" Stephen's hesitation stopped Richard from walking towards the house.

"Stephen? What's up?"

"Matthias was awake a while ago and I got some broth down him. He's hurting badly, Richard, in more ways than one. Do you know they kept him shackled every day? I don't think he's eaten much either from what he's said. He should be in a hospital."

"I know and we can't chance that. What else?"

"He never saw his kidnappers, but he thinks they deliberately left the door unlocked that last night, to try and track him. I've gone over his clothes." Stephen held out a hand. "I found this."

Richard reached for it. "A GPS tracker."

Stephen nodded. "That means they know where we are."

Richard sighed. "It does. Can he travel?"

"If we have to."

"We will. Go, pack up your stuff. We're heading out of here. Pray we're in time. Leave this in the bedroom. You're sure it's the only one?"

"I am."

Larkin watched as Matthias was carried to the SUV and tucked inside, before she was tucked into another one.

"What's going on, Naomi?"

"Whoever kidnapped Matthias put a tracker on him. We have to move."

Larkin's face whitened. "How long do we do this? And how does this hurt Matthias?"

"Richard's aware of how it can hurt him, but it would hurt you more if they found you. Now, hush, do your seatbelt up. We're moving."

Minutes after they drove away, two large vans stopped and men piled out, heading for the house. They stopped in frustration after the search, realizing Larkin had gotten away. The leader reached for the tracker, realizing that their scheme had failed. How was he to report back to his

leader they had failed once more? Who was
fighting this battle for her anyway?

Chapter 21

Matthias finally stirred, his eyes blinking open as he tried to focus. It wasn't the same room, he thought. He moved his head, finding the headache had lessened. He still didn't know what day it was. He felt a gentle hand on his face and turned, his eyes squinting as he tried to focus.

"Larkin? Is that you?" Matthias' voice was rough and he had to swallow a couple of times to be able to speak.

"It is. Here, let's get some water down you." She propped his head up and held the glass to his mouth, waiting until he swallowed some. "Not too much right at first. I'll give you some more in a few minutes." She set the glass back on the table, then watched as Matthias moved restlessly.

"Where are we, Larkin?"

"With friends, Matthias. Somehow, you got away and Bill made arrangements for you to join me and Richard's team."

"I don't get it. How?"

"No one seems to know. But you're here. Stephen's looking after you and you're finally awake."

Larkin's hand found Matthias' and held it as she watched. He tried hard to stay awake, but she saw him lose the battle and slip away from her once more. She turned at a sound from the doorway.

Stephen stood and watched. "He was awake?"

"He was and he was speaking. I'm not sure how much he remembers though."

"That's okay, Larkin. He'll not likely remember much, which may be a blessing in disguise. I need you to go and get some food. I'll let you back to see him in a couple of hours."

She nodded, knowing the routine. "Thank you, Stephen." She hesitated, her eyes on Matthias, then turned and walked from the room.

Bill looked around as he heard his name called and stood from the table he had been working at.

"Andrew? I didn't expect to see you today."

"I just got an email from Richard. He said he had sent you one as well but hadn't heard back from you." Andrew handed him the papers he had been holding. "Larkin's been busy."

Bill scanned the papers. "I see that. This is great. She's given me more names to follow through. I had some of them but not all that she's come up with." He stopped, his face thoughtful. "Have you talked to the judge?"

"I have. We're good to go with the warrants once you have your team assembled and the investigation to the point we can ask for the warrants. How long do you figure?"

"A couple of days with what I have, but now Larkin's come through with more names, it may be another day." He scanned the room, then called for Sid. "Sid, here. There are some names on this we didn't have. Work your magic for me."

"With pleasure.   Andrew, anything else?"

"No.   It looks as Bill has everything under control."   He grinned at the choked-back laugh from Bill. "Come find me if you need me."

Andrew walked back to his office, thoughts dark as he considered what he needed to do next.   He sighed as he looked at his desk.   He needed a break and just couldn't seem to catch one. He looked back the way he had come and said a prayer for his detectives, asking for guidance and wisdom for them, before shutting his door and sinking down into his chair.

An email from a friend in another jurisdiction caught his attention. What did Amos want, he wondered? Reading it, he sat back, considering what he should do. He knew he had vacation time coming up, but this request was urgent.   He needed the trouble with Larkin over and over yesterday. He sighed, typed out his response, and then picked up his phone. He needed to talk to his captain.

Richard strode through the house, on the hunt for Stephen. Not seeing him, he headed outside.

"Stephen? How's Matthias?"

"Getting better every hour. His headache is pretty much gone and he's been up on his feet."

"That's good news. I heard from Bill. He wants us to bring them back to Elmton."

Stephen spun to stare at him. "Back to Elmton?"

"That's what he said. He's about ready to serve warrants, and wants those two close to where he is so he can talk to them in person before he serves the warrants." He sighed. "I don't like it. I don't think it's the way to go."

"I don't either, not given what we just ran from. Does he have a safe place for them?"

"Not that I know of. He mentioned that the names Larkin provided at the last make a big difference in their investigation." He turned in a circle. "There's someone out there, Stephen. Pull everyone back to the house and get ready to move."

“Will do.” Stephen ran for the house as Richard headed for the SUVs.

“We’re on the move again, people. Leave everything and hit the vehicles.”

Matthias grabbed Larkin’s hand and followed Stephen, sliding into the backseat with Larkin beside him. He watched as the SUVs sped away from the house and headed towards Elmton.

Richard turned to watch behind them, listening to something on his radio. Then he pointed.

“There, Stephen. We made it out of there just in time. How did they find us?”

“I have no idea. I’ve searched everything I can to find trackers. We even went over the vehicles.”

“Somehow, they found us. Take us around Elmton and for Oak City. I’m not taking a chance on going through there.” He pulled out his phone. “Bill? They found us again. I have no idea how. No, I’m not heading for Elmton. I’m not saying where we’ll be. I’ll be in touch.” He disconnected the call on Bill’s protest and pocketed it.

"Now, where in Oak City?" Stephen shot him a look, then checked the two sitting behind him.

"I think we need to split up first. Naomi, your vehicle heads for Riverville. I'll send you details as to where we are. If we split, maybe we can throw them off."

Richard watched as the other SUV shot away from them, taking another road. Stephen headed for Oak City, then cut around it at Richard's request.

"I don't see anyone following us, Richard."

"I don't either." Richard turned to stare behind them, then shot a quick look at Matthias and Larkin. "We're trying to find somewhere safe for you two, at least for the next couple of days, until Bill serves his warrants. It's getting more difficult as the ones after you get more desperate."

Matthias nodded. "Where were you thinking?"

"We've done rural, we've done town. They've found us in both places."

"If we head for a downtown area, ditch your SUV for now, and head out on foot, maybe we can avoid them."

Richard turned to face the front of the vehicle once more, thinking about what Matthias had said.

"He's got a point there, Richard. We can always find another vehicle." Stephen glanced over at Richard.

"I know we can. Just, do we want to or do we have time?" His fingers tapped on the door, then he spoke. "Head for the shelter. I'll call in a favour with a friend, get us a new vehicle and hide this one for now."

"Andrew, we've got a problem." Bill appeared at Andrew's door.

"What now?"

"Richard's group was found. They've split up. Richard has the two with him. We need to get those warrants and get them served."

"The judge is waiting for you. Get moving. Let me know when you're back. I'll have your team ready for you."

Andrew rose and strode for the boardroom, his eyes searching for those he needed. He quickly gave directions and the men and women scattered to gather their equipment and everything else they needed to be ready when Bill returned.

Andrew watched, then sighed. Lord is this it?   Will this end it for Matthias and Larkin?

Back with the warrants, Bill divided his team, sending a detective with each group of officers. There would be a lot of overtime, but it would be worth it, he thought.

Chapter 22

Larkin paced, not knowing what was happening. Richard had finally tucked them away in an apartment near the downtown area of Oak City. Matthias watched as she paced, knowing how stressed she was.

Lord, we need this to end. Please, Lord. Larkin can't take much more. Matthias turned as he heard the door open and saw Richard coming back in.

"Richard?" Larkin spun to stare at him. "What happened?"

Richard drew a deep breath. "It's over, Larkin. They've got them all, including the leader. We're taking you two home."

Larkin stood, hands covering her mouth. "It's over?"

Richard nodded. "It is, Larkin. We'll stay here tonight, then head for Elmton tomorrow. Bill and Andrew have gotten everyone."

Matthias approached Larkin and wrapped her in his arms. "You can go home, Larkin. Thank you, Lord."

She clung to him, sobs shaking her body. "Thank you, Matthias."

He just hugged her tighter, nodding at Richard as he turned and walked back out the door.

Bill stood in the boardroom, looking over all the paperwork. Andrew found him.

"You've done good once again, Bill. Do we have everyone?"

"We do, Andrew. That we do. I'm so thankful for Larkin's and Matthias' sake. I would never have expected the ones we arrested though."

"No. I wouldn't either. You're working through the interrogations?"

"Our detectives are. Most have asked for lawyers, but we have enough that we can explain it to Larkin and Matthias." He turned to stared at his friend. "I never expected that the town accountant would be the one at the head of it all."

"No. He hid it well. Larkin pegged him, though, with tracing through the families."

"I'll be interested in hearing the results of his interrogations. I'm sure he'll blame someone else."

"We have too much evidence to tie him in." Bill studied Andrew. "You're exhausted, Andrew. Are you taking some time off?"

"I am. I'll be heading out the end of next week for about three weeks. Get lots of rest, Bill. I'm leaving you in charge. The Captain approved it."

"Andrew!" Bill watched as Andrew walked away, his laughter floating behind him, before he turned back to his task, shaking his head.

Andrew headed for the boardroom the next morning, knowing Richard had brought Larkin and Matthias there. He nodded at Bill who stood waiting for him.

"We're ready with the details?" Andrew took the folder Bill handed him and opened it to scan the documents.

"We are. The accountant had finally talked when he found out the people he hired were talking to get lighter sentences. His reasons are really bizarre."

"I see that." Andrew looked at Bill, assessing where he was at. "Are you ready?"

"As ready as I'll ever be. I just wish it hadn't happened this way for those two."

"The Lord alone knows why, but my gut tells me Larkin wouldn't have found her hope again without going through this."

"That could well be." Bill opened the door and walked through, Andrew on his heels.

Both men studied the couple waiting for them, seeing the peace on their faces.

"Bill? Andrew?" Larkin's voice was quiet.

"Larkin. Matthias. It's over. He's talking." Bill slid into a chair facing them.

Matthias' arm tightened around Larkins' shoulder. "It's over, finally?"

Andrew nodded. "It is. Give us a bit to bring you up to date, and then we'll take you home."

Bill spoke. "This is what we have. You were right on, Larkin, when you pegged Tam Forrester, the town accountant. He's the head of this group and has been for years. He would choose a paramedic group, such as yours, and put someone on the inside. That person would submit fraudulent claims for a certain period of time and then leave the group, moving from town. Then someone else would move into another group. He admitted putting Eve into your group. Somehow, she filed something wrong, and both you and Matthias ended up with the referral, which you shouldn't have. That led to this investigation and his downfall."

"It was him all along?" Larkin sat back, her arms folded across her stomach. "I never liked him, or his family for that matter. There was always a sense of evil around them."

"Your sense of who they are was right on. We've arrested his sons, his daughter, his nephews, and a cousin. They're the ones who were after you. Apparently he put a contract out of you, to have you taken out because he knew you had found out and wouldn't let it rest until you got to the bottom of it. Matthias was never to have been involved but Eve again sent him the referral when she shouldn't have."

Andrew spoke up. "We can't thank you two enough for being brave enough to follow through at risk to your lives and limbs. You've solved a mystery that has been bothering the police department here for years. In fact, you helped solve a cold case for us."

"We did?" Matthias looked at Larkin, then at Bill and Andrew. "How?"

"Larkin, do you remember about ten years ago the death of the homeless man, Fred, in a hit and run?" At her nod, Bill continued, "Fred had been hired by Forrester to apply for health benefits and then use a fraudulent group to put in for the money, which he turned over to Forrester. When his conscience got the better of him and he refused to cooperate any more, Forrester had him killed."

"Wow, that far back?" Larkin's eyes were round with wonder.

"That far back and even farther back. We still have a ways to go to finalize everything, but he's off the street and that portion of town has been cleaned up. Thanks to you two. Whoever was watching you, tried to kill you, set the bombs, owned the building, set up the letters, it all ties back to Forrester. You got involved because Eve made a mistake she paid for with her life."

Larkin shook her head. "No, it was your force who investigated and did the leg work. It's thanks to them and Don and Richard that we're still alive."

Andrew stood, reaching to shake their hands. "However it happened, you two can now go home. Richard said he'd be glad to play chauffeur one last time for you."

Matthias reached to draw Larkin into a hug. "It's over, sweetheart. We need to celebrate."

"First you need to rest. You're still a patient, you know." She leaned back to look up at him. "Give yourself a few days and then ask me again. I just might say yes." A sparkle of mischief lit her eyes.

"I'll do just that. Come on, sweetheart. Let's get Richard to take us to our homes."

Epilogue

Four months later, Matthias stood once more on the riverbank, his arms around Larkin. Over the past months, they had spent many hours together, getting to know one another, to find out who they each really were. Larkin's trust and hope in the Lord had grown by leaps and bounds, now that the burdens she had carried were gone. Matthias had finally gotten her to admit that she had suspected Forrester and his sons but with no proof, had not known who to talk to, not sure who they were paying off.

"This is just so peaceful, Larkin. I think this has become one of my favourite spots."

Larkin nodded, then rested her head back on Matthias' chest. "It has become one of mine as well. I love to watch the water flow and listen to the music it makes. Its moods reminds me so much of how God is with us no matter what we face. He calms

263

all our storms and walks through them with us."

"He does, sweetheart. I can see the change in you, the peace you now have."

She turned in his arms, her eyes studying his. "You've grown as well. When I first met you, I wasn't too sure about you or if I even wanted to talk to you."

"And now?" He looked down at her, a question in his eyes.

"Now, you're my best friend, I would have to say. It's not just what we went through together that makes it true. It's who you are and the leadership you show in our friendship."

Matthias nodded even as he bit his lip in uncertainty. Larkin's head tilted, as she watched him.

"Larkin, I know we've known each other for a while now, but what we went through brought us closer together than even an ordinary friendship would." He reached into a pocket and keeping his hand closed, released her, dropping to one knee in front of her.

She watched, hands to her mouth, as he opened his hand to show her a beautiful diamond and ruby ring.

"Larkin, will you be mine forever? Walk with me through this life? Be my soul mate and helpmeet? Will you be my wife, my love, my sweetheart for life?"

Tears glistened in her eyes as she nodded, then watched him slip the ring on her finger before rising and folding her to him, his lips seeking hers.

"Oh, Matthias. I thought I would live my life on my own, never having that one person God meant for me. You're him. God granted my deepest wish." This earned her another long kiss before he held her close to his heart.

"Don't make me wait too long, sweetheart."

They turned as the setting sun caught their eye and they basked in the glory God sent that night.

Dear Readers:

Thank you for reading the story of Larkin and Matthias and their adventures. They had quite the adventure, I must say.

Hope can be crushed so easily and it's so hard to find again when it is. What hope of yours has been crushed? I find solace in the fact that God is with me each day as I walk through life. When I have no hope, He is my hope. He restores me in ways I would never have thought.

As you travel through life, look around you. There are people out there who have lost their hope, their reason to live, whatever it is that keeps them going. We need to reach out as Christ would have done. How can you help? Pray that God uses you in a way you never expected. You'll not be surprised by how He does. Be that blessing to someone else and in doing that, you yourself are blessed.

Thank you once more for reading through this series. I've been taught so much myself by my characters. There are still four books to go in this series, and

Police Lieutenant Andrew certainly calling
for his own story.

God bless each one of you.

Ronna

www.ingramcontent.com/pod-product-compliance
Lightning Source LLC
Chambersburg PA
CBHW060914210726
48293CB00006B/2103